Jaws of Terror

Jaws of
Terror

Dayle Courtney

**Illustrated by
John Ham**

STANDARD PUBLISHING
Cincinnati, Ohio   2895

Thorne Twins Adventure Books

Library of Congress Cataloging in Publication Data

Courtney, Dayle.
  Jaws of terror.

  (Thorne Twins adventure books; 10)
  Summary: Eric's Christian values help him and his friend
Tom as they try to solve the mystery of Tom's father's disap-
pearance in a boat off the California coast years before.
  [1. Mystery and detective stories. 2. Twins—Fiction. 3.
Christian life—Fiction] I. Ham, John, ill. II. Title. III. Series:
Courtney, Dayle. Thorne Twins adventure books; 10.
PZ7.C83158Jaw   [Fic]   82-5511
ISBN 0-87239-554-5   AACR2

4

Contents

1 • *Mysterious Disappearance*

The eight-foot shark was swimming toward him.

Eric Thorne felt shivers along his neck as the sleek, powerful body came closer. He could see the cold black eyes, the rows of pointed teeth. Now something else moved above him—another shark—a hammerhead, coming fast. Beyond it were other dark shapes like shadows in the water, all with the unmistakable triangular dorsal fin held rigid, all moving with lethal grace in a kind of aquatic ballet.

Eric felt his throat muscles constricting. The nearest shark was close enough now that he could see tiny holes pockmarking its snout above nostrils that widened slightly, as though it were trying to catch scent of him. Repulsed, he moved back and felt a tug at his arm.

"Quite a display, isn't it?" the man beside him said.

The spell broken, Eric grinned at his Uncle Walter. "Sure is! I'm glad there's safety glass between us and those sharks!"

The huge shark tank occupied one whole room of this Sea World exhibit, where a crowd of people watched the fish and listened to a Sea World guide talking about them. "It's a cartilaginous fish—that means its entire body is made up of cartilage. Because of this, it's very hard to determine the age of a shark. We don't know how old these sharks are, and we don't know how old sharks live to be . . ."

The big fish swam ceaselessly around the large tank. The voice of the girl at the microphone echoed through the room, while music thrummed an eerie accompaniment to her words. Eric and his uncle stood by the railing near the glass and stared with the rest of the spectators.

It was strange, Eric thought, how everyone seemed to find these dangerous fish so fascinating. Was it because of the books and movies about them? Or was it something about the sharks themselves—the very fact that some of them had killed human beings? Whatever the reason, the shark exhibit was attracting a big crowd.

The girl at the microphone stopped talking and the music rose. Most of the crowd moved away from the tank to ask questions of the guide or go on to another exhibit. But one woman still stood by the railing. Eric glanced casually toward her, then found it hard to look away.

She was as beautiful as a movie star. Her long black hair curled over the shoulders of the crimson dress she wore, and her complexion was very fair. She leaned forward a little, as though she would like to join the sharks that swam in the tank. She watched them intently. A young man about Eric's age stood beside her.

"That's Kara Kelsey." Uncle Walter was looking at her, too. "She's working for her doctorate in marine biology at Scripps. Even taking a few of my classes. Come on, we'll go say hello to her."

The teenager beside her noticed them as they approached. Eric thought he looked golden-brown all over, with his sandy hair, light brown eyes, and lightly-tanned skin. A sprinkling of brown freckles covered his nose and cheeks, and he even wore a light brown T-shirt over his brown cords. He nudged the woman beside him. "Mom!"

She didn't seem to hear him, or even to be conscious he was there. Her whole attention was on the sharks.

Uncle Walter held out his hand to the young man. "How are you, Tom? I haven't seen you since last summer." Then he turned to the woman. "Kara?"

Slowly she turned around, obviously reluctant to tear her gaze away from the sharks, and it was a moment before recognition replaced her dreamy expression and she smiled. "Dr. Thorne!"

"Walter, please. No need to be formal, especially when we're not in the classroom. And I'd like you both to meet my nephew, Eric Thorne, who's spending the summer with me. He's interested in marine biology."

Kara Kelsey held out her hand to Eric. "I can see the family resemblance," she said. "The same dark, curly hair. The same blue eyes. And you're nearly as tall as your uncle."

"I'm five-eleven. I've still got a couple of inches to go before I'm his height." Now that Eric was closer to her he could see that she was older than he'd first thought. She had to be thirty-seven or so, about the same age as his uncle. Her large eyes were greenish-blue like the sea, and although she smiled with the rest of her face, he could see something strange and cold in them. When she shook his hand, hers felt cool and smooth.

But Tom's handshake was as warm and hearty as the grin he gave Eric. "You like scuba diving?" he asked. "Just got some equipment. Going to go diving as soon as I can."

"Sure," Eric said. "I've done some diving."

Uncle Walter was talking to Kara. "Interesting exhibit, isn't it?"

She nodded. "Beautiful!"

"Beautiful?" His dark eyebrows raised and he gave her a questioning smile. "Well, I don't know about beautiful. I don't think sharks are as pretty as garibaldi or butterfly fish, for instance." His tone was gently teasing, and Eric noticed the way he looked at this woman, as though he thought her even more attractive than the fish he was talking about.

Kara spoke quickly, changing the subject. "I wanted Tom to see this. He just came back from Seattle yesterday. The last time he visited Sea World must have been when he was only ten or eleven."

Eric felt restless. He didn't want to stand here and listen to them make small talk, not when there were so many more interesting things to see. "Did you see the prehistoric jaws outside?" he asked Tom.

"No. Where?"

"Come on, I'll show you." He led the way down a corridor toward the rest of the shark exhibit. "Are you going to school up in Seattle?"

"Yeah, I'm finishing high school there, where my grandparents live. Then I'll come back here and go to college. Where do you go to school?"

"In Ivy, Illinois. That's where I live. Do you do any surfing?"

"Sure. Do you?"

"There's no place to surf around Ivy," Eric said, "but I've been surfing in Hawaii. It was great. Haven't done any here yet. Only got here last night, and today my uncle wanted to show me the sights. It looks like there's good surf out by his house."

"Right," Tom said. "He lives a couple of blocks from our house. We're right near the beach. We could go out sometime, if you like."

"Sure." Eric was glad to meet someone his own age here. He hated to admit it, but already he missed his twin sister, Alison. They usually traveled together, but this time she'd decided to spend her vacation working on her piano lessons, since she hoped to perform in a concert in September.

They were standing in front of the life-size model of the jaws of an enormous white shark when the two adults joined them.

"Look at those, Mom!" Tom pointed out. "A prehistoric shark's jaws. They look big enough to demolish a dinosaur."

Kara studied the model and Eric noticed that her face took on a look of intense interest, just as it had when she watched the sharks in the tank. She was almost smiling, as though she shared some secret with these fish that no one else could know.

Tom sighed impatiently and moved away. There was

11

a brief silence while Eric wondered if anyone could really admire sharks as much as she seemed to.

Walter Thorne cleared his throat. "Unlike other species, sharks haven't changed much through the centuries. They seem to be just about the same now as they were thousands of years ago." And then, as she turned to him, he smiled at her. "Eric and I were going to have dinner at Limehouse. Would you and Tom like to join us?"

She shook her head quickly. "I don't think so . . ." she began, but Tom, standing in front of the adjoining exhibit, had heard the invitation. "That sounds great!"

"No," Kara said firmly. "Not today. But thank you anyway." She turned and began to walk away.

Tom hung back uncertainly as though he wanted to say something more, then grinned ruefully at Eric. "I'll be over tomorrow morning early to go surfing."

"Okay. See you then."

"You got a surfboard?" Tom asked, as an afterthought. "If not, I've got two."

"I'll need to borrow one until I can get my own."

"Okay. See you." He strode after his mother and both of them disappeared in the crowd outside.

Uncle Walter was shaking his head. "Strange woman, Kara Kelsey. A real puzzle." He and Eric walked slowly through the doorway leading outside. "She keeps to herself. There are lots of us who'd like to be friends with her, but she won't have anything to do with any of us."

"Tom seems like a nice guy," Eric said.

"Maybe he's more like his father than his mother. I don't know. I never knew his father."

12

"What happened to him?"

"He disappeared a long time ago. He o[...]
in partnership with another man. It's righ[...]
Jolla. They sell boats, repair them, and rent [...]
space for them. I guess Kara still owns an int[...]
and she still lives in the same house, but her h[...] and
disappeared before I came here. Kara and Tom went
away a few years ago, but then they came back here so
she could resume her studies at Scripps. That's about
all I know about them." Uncle Walter stroked his dark,
curly beard thoughtfully. "It might be the tragedy in her
life—her husband's disappearance, I mean—that makes
her the way she is."

They walked across the bridge outside that spanned
the pools where the smaller sharks were kept, and went
through the crowd of sightseers toward the main gate.
"But how did Tom's father disappear?" Eric asked.

"The way I heard it, he went out on his boat one
night and never came back."

"And they never found his body or the boat?"

"I don't believe so. Now, shall we go get some
Chinese food, or would you rather eat my bachelor-type
cooking tonight?"

"I have a yen for Chinese," Eric said.

Although it was after ten o'clock when they got back
to Walter Thorne's comfortable, modern house in La
Jolla, Eric went to the telephone in the kitchen to call
his father. It would be midnight in Ivy, but he knew Dad
often worked late and would be anxious to hear that
he'd arrived in California safely. He was surprised
when Alison answered the phone.

13

'Well," she said in her sternest tone, "it's about time you got around to phoning. We were just beginning to think you'd forgotten all about us. Out of state, out of mind, as the saying goes." Even though Alison was Eric's twin, she often spoke to him as though she were older—which, of course, she was, by twenty minutes.

Eric grinned, picturing her as she must look now, frowning as she scolded him. "I've been having too much fun to stop and call you," he said. "You don't know what you're missing! We went to Sea World today, and tomorrow I'll be out on a surfboard riding the wild waves . . ."

"If you're trying to make me jealous, Eric Thorne, you can forget it. We're having lots of fun here, too. Gramps has invited us to a dinner at the White House in July that you'll have to miss, and I just came home from Belinda's graduation party. It was absolutely fantastic. Too bad you couldn't be there. All the girls were asking about you."

Uncle Walter, who was getting iced tea from the refrigerator, saw Eric's grin. "Is that Alison? Tell her my invitation still stands if she wants to come here for the summer."

Eric relayed the message to his sister.

"No. I can't. But I'd love to see him again. Can I say hello to him?"

"Sure." Eric handed the phone to his uncle, who talked to Alison and then to Eric's father.

"How are you, Randy? How's the research going? Glad to hear it. Important work. We'll have to compare notes on soil conservation and marine resources next time we're together."

14

The conversation went on for a few minutes, then Eric heard his name mentioned. "He's fine. Grown up so much I hardly recognized him at the airport. Yes, it'll be great having him here. He's good company. And even though I'll only be free on weekends, I know Eric will enjoy himself. There's a nice kid practically next door to us named Tom Kelsey. He and Eric met today and seemed to hit it off very well. But here, you can talk to Eric yourself."

Dr. Randall Thorne's voice on the phone was warm and familiar. "How are you, Eric? How was the trip?"

"Fine, Dad. No problems at all."

"Did Walter mention the name Kelsey?"

"Right. Tom Kelsey. We met him and his mother today at Sea World."

His dad sounded excited. "I wonder if that's Stephen Kelsey's son? I knew Steve back in the sixties. Admired his work a great deal. He was very well known in environmental circles, you know."

"I'm not sure what Tom's father's name was, Dad. Uncle Walter said he disappeared years ago, and that he never knew him."

"I'm positive that would be Steve Kelsey. Disappeared under very mysterious circumstances. Nobody ever found out what happened to him, but a lot of people have their own ideas."

"What do they think happened?" Eric asked.

"Oh, I think they're just speculating. I don't want to repeat half-truths and gossip, Eric. But Steve was doing some very important research, and all of his records disappeared at the same time he did. You know how people talk."

15

The rest of their conversation concerned family matters. Eric talked with Aunt Rose before he hung up, and promised to keep in touch.

Afterwards, he and his uncle started a game of chess, but Eric soon found himself yawning. The sea air and the change in time had tired him, so he decided to turn in. His room was a wood-paneled guest room with wide windows that overlooked the moonlit sea, and soon the sound of the waves had lulled him into a deep sleep.

Tom phoned at dawn the next morning, sounding excited. "Eric, Mom and I are going out on our boat. She's got some research to do and she says you're welcome to come along with us. We can go scuba diving."

"Great! I'll check with my uncle and call you back." Eric went searching for Uncle Walter and found him sitting on the small, flower-decked terrace of the house, looking at the ocean through a pair of binoculars. "You're up early," Eric said. "I thought you might still be asleep."

"I like to come here and watch the sea in the early morning." He handed Eric the binoculars. "Look out there. Gray whales."

Through the powerful lenses, Eric could see the huge mammals outlined against the pale horizon, plumes of spray rising from blowholes; mammoth tails waving as they dove in and out of the dark waves.

"The last stragglers migrating north," his uncle said.

"They're huge."

"Right. Huge and harmless."

"Maybe I can get a close up view of them. Mrs.

Kelsey's invited me to go with her and Tom this morning while she does some research. Tom says we can go scuba diving."

Walter Thorne gave a surprised whistle. "I can't believe it! She's actually inviting a stranger? Oh . . . I get it. You'll be good company for Tom. Well, consider yourself uniquely favored."

"I'd feel better if she'd invited you, too," Eric said.

"Don't worry about me. I've got plenty to keep me busy right here. You go and have a good time."

After he'd phoned Tom, Eric went to his room, put on swimming trunks and a T-shirt, and in a few minutes Tom was there to pick him up. After bidding his uncle good-bye, the two boys got into a yellow MGB convertible parked at the curb.

"This yours?" Eric asked. "Neat little car."

"It's mine to use for the summer," Tom said. "It's really my mother's second car. We're supposed to meet her at the marina. They're getting the boat ready there." He pulled the car away from the curb.

"Is that the marina your father owned?" Eric asked.

"Yes. How did you know?"

"My uncle told me, and when I talked with my dad last night he said he knew your father a long time ago. That is, if his name was Stephen Kelsey."

The little car swerved suddenly as Tom turned to Eric with a look of agitation on his face.

"Hey!" Eric grabbed at the side door as he jolted in the seat.

"Sorry." Tom regained control of the car, but Eric could see he was very disturbed.

"What's the matter?"

"You said your father *knew* my father?"

"Yeah. Said he was very well known among people like my dad who work to save the environment."

Tom didn't seem to believe this. "He was?"

"Didn't you know that?"

Tom shook his head, keeping his eyes on the road as he turned the corner and pulled onto La Jolla Shores Drive. "I don't know very much about my dad. He disappeared when I was just a baby."

"But didn't your mother tell you?"

Tom glanced at him with sad, bewildered eyes. "Mom doesn't talk about Dad much. I guess it hurt her a lot when he went away." He took a deep breath before he spoke again. "What else did your father say about him?"

Eric tried to remember everything. "Not much. Just that your dad disappeared under mysterious circumstances, and that his work was very important."

The MG swerved again, then resumed its steady course. "You mean his work at the marina?"

"No. I think Dad was talking about his work as an environmentalist."

"Did he say what that work was?"

"No."

"Do you think he could tell you, if you asked him?"

"I'm not sure," Eric said. "Dad works with the International Agricultural Foundation, and sometimes he gets involved with secret government work that he can't really talk about. Maybe your father was, too. But I can ask Dad next time I talk to him, if you'd like."

Tom seemed very eager. "How long before you'll be talking to him again?"

18

"Well—I guess I could call him tonight or tomorrow, if it's that important to you. Dad said he's going to be home in Ivy for the next couple of weeks before he has to leave again."

"I'd appreciate it."

For a little while they drove in silence, the cool ocean breeze tossing Eric's hair, the California sunshine warm on his face and his bare arms and legs. Then Tom turned the car down a short road toward the beach, and they passed through the steel mesh gates with the sign KELSEY MARINA over them.

He parked the car under a shadeless palm tree in the small parking lot. Down the hill, Eric could see the slips where various small boats were moored and the two large, barnlike buildings that stood on the shore. He started to get out of the car, but Tom laid a hand on his arm to stop him.

"Wait a minute, will you?"

"Sure." Eric sat back in the seat and waited, letting him take his time. Tom was obviously upset, and it was a little while before he spoke.

"Ever since I was old enough to know anything about it, I've wondered just what happened to my father— why he took off on his boat one night without telling Mom where he was going, and then nobody ever heard from him again."

"Didn't your mom ever try to find out? Didn't anybody ever search for him?"

"I guess the police did, and the Coast Guard. But they never found him or the boat. That's all I know. And Mom says . . ." he hesitated, looking embarrassed.

"What?" Eric was curious.

"Well, I guess she has her own ideas about what happened to him." Tom's face darkened. "But I don't think she's right. She couldn't be right."

It was obvious he didn't want to tell Eric what his mother's theories were. Eric didn't press the point.

"So I don't want anyone else to know about what I'm going to tell you," Tom continued. "Not even Mom, or your uncle."

"Then I won't say anything to anyone," Eric promised.

"Okay. The thing is, I want to find out what really happened that night. I want to start right now and find out everything I can." Tom's voice was as strained as his face. "For all anyone knows, Dad might be still alive somewhere. But if he isn't—I think somebody might have killed him."

2 • Terror in the Kelp Bed

Eric stared at Tom, sitting next to him in the open car. "You think somebody might have killed your dad? But who? Why?"

"I don't know. That's what I've got to find out. The whole thing's been a mystery for too long. It's time somebody tried to solve it, and that somebody has to be me."

"But how are you going to find out anything?" It's been such a long time . . ."

"Sixteen years. But your father still remembers him, Eric. Maybe he can give me information that might help. And there must be other people—friends my dad had. Maybe they're still around and can give me clues."

Eric thought it over. It made a lot of sense. If he were in Tom's place, he'd feel the same way. His first impulse was to offer to help Tom, but did he want to spend his vacation that way? After all, it didn't have anything to do with him. And what help could he be, except to ask Dad for more information on Stephen Kelsey? And it wasn't as though Tom were an old friend.

As he was thinking, he looked down the slope, through a space between the two buildings. He could see Kara Kelsey on a small motor launch, bending over some gear. In a moment she straightened and went to the side of the boat, where she stood staring out to sea in a pose Eric remembered. She had stood like that, eager and intense, when he'd first seen her as she watched the sharks in the Sea World tank. Today she wore shorts and a blouse that were the color of blood. Somehow that outfit seemed strangely out of place on this pastel day of pale sand and pale sea.

Tom saw her, too. "There's Mom, waiting for us. I guess we'd better get going."

But Eric was still thinking about what he'd said. "If you're going to try to find out about your dad, why don't you want her to know?"

Tom frowned. "Oh—I guess I'm just not as close to her as I used to be, because I've been away a lot at school. I don't know how she'd take it. Maybe she wouldn't want me to do it, and I don't want anybody to try to stop me now that I've made up my mind."

And there was another mystery, Eric thought as he got out of the car and followed Tom down the hill. *Kara Kelsey.* According to Uncle Walter, she didn't want anyone to get close to her. Maybe that's why Tom felt the way he did. It seemed there were two mysteries, and he liked mysteries. He liked Tom, too. If he helped Tom in his search, they might even find those missing records Dad talked about, that were so important. What better way could he spend his summer?

"Hey!" he called to Tom, quickening his stride to catch up with him. "You know it could be dangerous, don't you? I mean, if your dad was . . . killed . . . then whoever did it might still be around, and they sure won't like anyone investigating."

"Yeah, I know that. I'll just have to be careful."

"Okay," Eric said. "When do we start?"

Tom stopped and looked at him. He gulped, as though words were stuck in his throat. "How about tomorrow morning?"

"Right." Eric broke into a jog down the paved slope, breathing in the smell of salt water and fish. As he neared the buildings, he could see that the one to his left was a restaurant, called *The Gull's Nest*, while the other seemed to be a sales office attached to a large warehouse. Several types of seagoing craft rested inside the barn-like building, and various others were propped up on the concrete outside it.

Now he and Tom walked along the dock where the boats were moored. Chain link fencing separated them from the jetties that ran at right angles to the waterfront. There were easily a hundred boats here, each moored in one of the slips that lined the jetties on both sides. They were all sizes and shapes, bobbing on the swell. Beyond, in the channel that ran past a sea wall and out to the open ocean, Eric could see sailboats and cabin cruisers, fishing boats and catamarans.

Tom led the way to a gate marked "E," opened it, and led the way down the stairs and along the jetty. Mrs. Kelsey saw them coming and waved to them. She was talking to a stocky, muscular man who turned as they approached.

"Hi, Al," Tom called to him.

"Well, well!" Al grinned. "I hardly recognized you. Can this be little Tom Kelsey, all grown up?"

Tom went up to him, hand outstretched. "Sure is."

Al enclosed Tom's hand in two big, ruddy fists, jerking it up and down. "You've grown as fast as a stalk of seaweed, son, but you're just as skinny." He pinched Tom's arm. "Have to get some meat on those bones."

Tom laughed and gave Al a friendly pinch on his own bulging biceps. "There's *meat* and then there's *blubber!*"

"Honest labor gave me this physique, son. But don't give up. It's something you can shoot for."

Mrs. Kelsey was watching the exchange with an amused look. "You haven't seen Tom since last summer, have you, Al?"

"Not since he decided to go to school up north with the Eskimos." Al winked at Tom.

"Eric, I'd like you to meet Al Madow," Tom said. "Al, this is Eric Thorne."

Al gave Eric a hearty handshake, then reached for a camera hanging on a strap around his neck. "I've been taking pictures of Jim Feiger and a fifteen-foot tuna he just caught. How about if I take one of you and your friend, Tom? The old one I've got on the office wall doesn't even look like you any more."

"Sure." Tom and Eric posed for the picture, smiling.

"I'm going to be around all summer," Tom said. "How about taking us out tuna fishing sometime soon?"

"Well," Al passed his hand through his thinning dark hair, "I've been as busy as a one-armed paperhanger lately, but sure, come on over, and I'll see what I can do."

"How about tomorrow?"

"We'll see," Al said. "Talk to me in the morning." He waved to the three of them and walked on down the jetty.

Eric and Tom boarded the trim motor launch and seated themselves on padded seats in the stern. Looking over the side, Eric could see the name *Remora* painted in red letters on it.

Mrs. Kelsey seemed impatient to leave, for she had the boat moving out of the marina almost as soon as they'd settled themselves.

Tom spoke to Eric in a low voice. "We can start with Al."

"What do you mean?"

"You know. The search. Al and Dad were partners at the time Dad disappeared."

Eric glanced at Mrs. Kelsey, who was steering the boat. She couldn't have heard from where she was sitting. Tom's words would have been lost under the sound of the motor. But she was looking at Eric now, and beckoning to him. He moved to stand beside her.

"Have you done any scuba diving before?" she asked.

"Oh, sure. Several times. Dad took my sister and me diving in the Mediterranean, and once we went in the Red Sea."

She glanced up at him. "Sounds like you've traveled a lot."

"My dad's work takes him all over the world, Mrs. Kelsey, so my sister and I have gone with him whenever and wherever we could, to keep the family together as much as possible."

"Don't call me *Mrs*. Kelsey." She sounded irritated. "I'm not *Mrs*. Not any more. You can call me Kara." She looked straight ahead, her chin set stubbornly.

How could he have annoyed her just by calling her Mrs. Kelsey? Eric was bewildered. But then, this woman was not easy to understand. She was certainly unlike anyone he'd ever met before.

"Does your mother travel with you?" she was asking, in a gentler tone.

"She died in a car accident when we were very young."

"I'm sorry to hear that. You and Tom have something in common, then."

Eric nodded. "Where are we heading?" he asked her.

"The kelp beds, not far from here."

"Is that where you're doing your research?"

She nodded. "There's a lot of change going on in the coastal waters of California. Part of my work is to keep records of exactly what's happening."

Eric didn't understand. "How could a bed of seaweed tell you anything?"

"A kelp bed is like an underwater city, full of marine life of all kinds. But the ecosystems are being affected by pollution, of course. Everything from the bacteria to the whale is suffering. Scientists at Scripps are recording the problems and trying to find solutions." She spoke crisply, impersonally, as the craft skimmed over the calm sea, while Tom sorted out the diving gear in the hold. Eric would have liked to ask her more, but her

26

manner was abrupt, as though she resented having to talk at all, and so he quietly watched the sunlight glinting on the water.

In about half an hour they reached a small, rocky island, where she cut the motor. Cormorants clung to folds of rock. Gulls wheeled around them. Eric smiled as he saw three brown pelicans scudding into a top-heavy landing on the island's pinnacle.

Kara began pulling her wetsuit over her shorts. "Even though you're both experienced, I'd like you to stay close to the surface. I'll be going to about a hundred foot depth, to measure the kelp I've tagged."

Tom helped her force her arms into the neoprene sleeves of the black suit, and while she finished dressing, he fitted the regulator on the neck of the air tank, checked the wing nut that held it in place, and opened the air valve. He sucked some air from the tank to be sure it was working properly, then held it while his mother slipped her arms through the straps and fastened the third strap around her waist.

"You remember how it goes, Tom? I'll send up red floats if I need any help. I've got enough air for about fifteen minutes."

"Right, Mom."

They watched as Kara spat into her face mask, rubbed saliva around on the glass, then fitted it over her eyes and nose. Then, with the mouthpiece of her air regulator in place, she sat on the edge of the deck and dropped backwards into the water. She waved her hand to them before she went under the surface, leaving only a few bubbles to mark where she had been.

"What was that about red floats?" Eric asked.

"That's one reason she asked us to stay close to the surface. If anything dangerous should happen down there, then she'll send up floats to let me know. Sometimes she gets so wrapped up in what she's doing that she forgets to watch her air pressure gauge or anything else."

They helped each other into their diving gear, Eric pulling on the flippers Uncle Walter had lent him. "If you're away at school most of the time, who usually comes with her?" he asked.

"Nobody. She doesn't ever go diving with anyone else. Just me."

"But I thought divers were always supposed to work on the buddy system—two at a time."

Tom shrugged, but it was obvious that he worried about her. And, Eric thought, maybe Uncle Walter worried about her, too. He'd seemed concerned that Kara had no friends and wanted none. Was he romantically attracted to Kara? Eric had noticed something in his manner that was more than a professor's interest in a student. But this thought passed as he strapped his air cylinder in place, put on his face mask, and flopped into the water after Tom.

He paddled experimentally for a time, staying close to the surface of the water, getting the feel of swimming once more with the unaccustomed weight of a tank and weight belt on his body. It took only a short while before he felt at home, breathing comfortably through his mouthpiece, his flippers thrusting him quickly downward.

At first he could see nothing but the taut white anchor line descending into darkness, and Tom's black-suited figure close by. Then he saw that they were over a kind of forest . . . a forest of seaweed. Sunlight filtered from the surface, casting a pale emerald light among the swaying fronds. Eric and Tom went down until they were swimming through the strands of giant kelp.

A school of silvery slapjacks darted past Eric's face. A distance away he saw flashes of bright orange and recognized them as garibaldi. Now he could see more colors—anemones and sea hares, and squid jet-propelling among them. As Kara had said, there was a whole city down here, Eric thought, inhabited by all kinds of fish and plants. He wished he could go down farther, to see more of them, but he remembered her request and stayed not far from the surface, enjoying the feeling of weightlessness and the novelty of this seaweed forest.

After a while, he noticed that he and Tom had become separated. Eric tried to find him among the thick growth of kelp, but after a few minutes he realized he'd have to give up. Tom could be anywhere. He might have even surfaced for some reason. Eric decided it would be best to do just that, and began his ascent, moving upward gradually as he had been taught, looking around for Tom as he went.

It was then he saw the shark. It looked huge as it moved swiftly toward him, filtered sunlight gleaming on its blue back, glinting off its rigid dorsal fin. A blue shark, not twenty feet away from him! Eric felt suddenly heavy—heavier than rock—heavier than a lump of iron. Heart pounding, he tried to force his arms and legs to carry him upward quickly, but it was like a bad dream, where his legs dragged uselessly and his arms were helpless. He was moving up, but so slowly! And the shark was coming toward him like a torpedo on target. Through a haze of fear, he saw a grouper dart crazily before the shark's pointed nose, and saw the great jaws open, showing lethal rows of razor-edged teeth, snapping the big fish inside.

He must have been holding his breath because suddenly he felt himself choking, the air pumping steadily into his mouth making him cough. His mouthpiece flew out and he gulped in seawater. But he couldn't move. The blue shark was still coming on, its cold eyes looking hungrily at him, and he could only wait. He closed his eyes, then opened them and saw the huge white belly swooping over him, like a giant bird in flight, so close to his head that he could reach out and touch it.

Now his hand unfroze, grabbed at his mouthpiece and set it back between his lips. He swallowed the air that spread through his body in a healing current as he struggled upward. He mustn't panic. He knew that. But it was hard to make his frantic limbs slow down. Anyway, he wasn't going to wait until that shark turned around and came back for him, no matter what. He wasn't even going to look and see where it was now. It must have been ten feet long! He wondered if Tom had seen it too. Or had *it* seen Tom first? He shoved that thought aside.

At last his head broke the water's surface, sunlight dazzling his eyes. He bobbed for a moment, looking around, trying to get his bearings. He could see he was perhaps fifteen feet away from the boat. Tom was nowhere in sight. Eric glanced toward the rocky island, but only the seabirds looked back at him. He turned, scanning the waters for any sign of sharks, relieved when he saw no fins . . . no sleek, swift shadows under the surface.

But now his mind raced, wondering if he should go back under to look for Tom, to warn him? If he did, he took a chance on meeting that blue again. Better swim for the safety of the boat. The shark could be far away by now. It was a big ocean, after all.

What if it still roamed the kelp bed and Tom might need his help? He'd have to go down again. And then there was Kara, who might be coming up at any time. These thoughts took just a fraction of a second, and he had just made up his mind that he would have to dive again when he saw a black-suited figure surfacing a few feet away, and Tom's freckled face turning toward him. With a wild wave of his hand, Tom streaked through the water toward the boat. Eric followed him, and it wasn't long before they were scrambling on board.

Tom's teeth were chattering. "Did you see them down there? Great big blue sharks?"

"I only saw one. There were more of them?"

"Three. I just about bumped into one before I saw it. Man! I never swam so fast in all my life!" His eyes widened as he looked out over the ocean, and his voice was a hoarse shout. "Look!"

Eric saw the shark fin cutting the water at just about the place where he and Tom had surfaced, and his heart began to pound. He stared wordlessly at it as it made a slow circle, not wanting to voice the thought that was uppermost in his mind now. Kara! Tom must be thinking of her, too. Both of them stood by the boat's rail, waiting, watching, knowing she would be surfacing

soon, dreading the moment when she would, yet dreading even more the possibility that she wouldn't. It had to be fifteen minutes since she went down. Time dragged on, and another fin joined the first, both of them circling around the boat like a deadly carousel.

"She said she'd send up red floats," Tom said quietly, never taking his gaze away from the sharks.

"And if she does? What'll you do?" It wasn't curiosity that made Eric ask. He had to steel himself now for whatever he might be called upon to do. But if there were three sharks, as Tom said, and she met one as she was coming up—what could anyone do?

Tom didn't answer, and Eric understood. It was a helpless feeling just standing there. The feeling increased as they waited, until the two cobalt fins on the sparkling water had etched themselves with razor sharpness into his eyes and mind.

"Mom!" The scream jolted Eric back to awareness.

Kara was surfacing. She squinted toward them.

"Mom! Hurry!" Tom waved and howled. "Sharks!"

She didn't seem to understand. She stared at them through her faceplate, treading water.

"Mom! Sharks!" Tom threw one leg over the rail of the boat, holding on with one hand while he pointed with the other. The two sharks were arching at the farthest side of their circle away from the boat. Kara would still have time to swim to safety.

Eric leaned over the rail, clenching it with his fingers. "Kara! Quick! Sharks in the water!"

She turned her head to look where Tom was pointing, then slowly she looked back at them. Eric couldn't believe what he saw.

She was smiling.

She waved one hand at them. It was a happy wave. "It's okay. Stay there. I'm fine." Even her voice, clear and distinct across the water, sounded pleased. Then, as Eric stared incredulously and Tom moaned with pain, she replaced her mouthpiece and dived under the surface of the water.

The two sharks were nearing the boat again, swimming toward the place where she had disappeared.

Tom gave an agonized howl and wriggled over the boat's rail. Eric grabbed his arm, trying to stop him.

"Let go!" Tom seemed to be hysterical now.

Eric tried to calm him. "She said not to panic. She'll be all right." He almost believed what he was saying.

"I've got to save her!" Tom struggled to free himself from Eric's grasp.

"She's all right. You'll see. She knows about sharks, remember?"

Tom turned his face to look at Eric with horrified, frightened eyes. "They'll tear her into bloody pieces. You saw those teeth! You know what they'll do to her!" He pulled his face mask down over his eyes and nose with his free hand, then gave a furious tug, lunging forward over the rail as he did so.

Eric, gripping Tom's arm stubbornly, felt himself slipping over the rail. Tom finally managed to tear his arm free of Eric's grasp, and as he plunged feet first into the ocean, Eric wildly tried to find a handhold to stop his forward lurch.

But it was too late. He was falling into the water, where the sharks were waiting.

3 • Shark!

He heard a sound like an explosion as he hit the water, then silence as he sank downward. He struggled frantically to stop himself, thrusting against the fall with flippers and arms, twisting his body. Something solid knocked against his chest, pushing him back, and he opened his eyes, terrified that he would see a shark. No, thank God, it wasn't a shark. It was Tom, his flippers thrashing, moving away in a halo of bubbles.

Eric swam furiously for the surface, every nerve in his body screaming. He couldn't think any more. He could only feel, and what he felt was dread. His chest was tight with lack of air. He tried to look everywhere at once, searching out his enemies.

When he surfaced, he gulped air quickly. Then, without looking around, he headed for the boat.

He had to make several tries before his shaking hands could pull his weight up onto the deck. Then he collapsed flat on his stomach, pressing his face against the safety of the wood, feeling the quick, heavy rhythm of his heartbeat.

The terror ebbed gradually. He was slowly aware of the sun's heat on his back; the slapping of the waves against the boat; the sound of his own breathing; the clamor of his thoughts. Tom and Kara were down there among the sharks.

Soon he was able to control himself and he stopped shaking and panting. He sat up and looked out at the water. No fins circling there, only dancing sparkles as waves caught sunlight.

He stood up quickly. He wasn't going to panic again. He would have to go down there. He had to help his friends—and himself. He couldn't let fear take charge of him, or it would grow until it stopped him from ever diving again. He settled his face mask in place and made sure his air cylinder was secure.

He felt a thrill of fear as he plunged into the water again. But it didn't last. He settled his mouthpiece between his jaws, forcing his movements to be calm, and then he dived.

The forest of kelp was barely visible below him. He sank gradually until he could see the sheen of distilled sunlight on the tops of the waving fronds. Then, moving cautiously, he began his search for the Kelseys.

It was like crawling through a cornfield, trying to find someone among the tall stalks, except for the schools of little fish that swarmed around him. He watched warily for the white underbellies and indigo backs of the sharks. But the undersea world was peaceful. None of the inhabitants seemed to be afraid, not even of this black-suited stranger who moved among them.

36

Finally Eric knew he would have to surface. He must have used nearly all his oxygen. Tom and Kara would be in the same situation. Surely they were back on the boat by now.

But as he rose above the seaweed, he saw the sharks. The pit of dread in his stomach opened again, but he forced himself to stay calm. They were maybe 20 feet away from him, two of them circling above, one following their movements a few feet below them. And he saw something else—something that sent prickles of fear along his spine. He reached for a strand of kelp to stop his rise, then stared at the sight.

Kara was swimming beside the lowest shark. Shafts of blue-green light glinted on her suit and on the sleek body of the shark as they glided weightlessly through the sunlit silence. She was swimming with graceful, languid movements, circling as the sharks circled. The sight was breathtakingly beautiful—and terrifying.

One of the sharks above her began to descend, heading for her, and Eric thought for one awful moment that it was going to stop her dance forever, but it passed and went under, then was lost in the dark forest below. Kara slowed and watched it, then turned her face upward and began to ascend.

Something bumped his arm. He turned quickly. It was Tom, grasping at Eric's shoulder with one hand, pointing toward Kara with the other. Then, with a thrust of his feet, he was swimming toward her. Eric followed, seeing the two sharks still cruising above her. She was rising to meet them, moving swiftly and confidently. The pit of dread in Eric's stomach widened. This couldn't be happening! It was too fantastic!

Tom, swimming quickly, was approaching his mother now, with Eric a few feet behind. And Kara saw them. She turned her face downward, looking toward them, as Tom's hand reached out for her ankle.

Eric watched, feeling as though it were all a dream. He couldn't even feel fear now; a numbness dulled his perceptions, so that what happened next seemed like a series of still pictures flickering on a silent screen.

Kara suddenly glanced up at the sharks, then back to Tom. She reached out for him in a protective gesture, an opening of the arms. Then she moved away from him, leading the way upward but away from the sharks. The stream of bubbles from her air supply became sporadic for a moment, then stopped. She beckoned to Tom and Eric, and continued. One of the blue sharks made a swift turn and headed for her. Kara moved unhurriedly toward the surface, the two boys following. Her movements were still graceful as the shark circled around the group of divers, so close at one time that Eric could see the movement of the five vertical gill slits on its side. He fought down the fear that rose in him. Kara was not afraid. He would not be afraid.

When the shark turned and came toward them again, Kara faltered. She needed air. But they were nearly at the surface. Tom came up behind her, grasped her around the waist and thrust her upward. At this sudden movement, the shark jerked around and came closer. Kara's head, then Tom's, broke the surface. Afraid of attracting the shark's attention, Eric stopped moving his arms and legs, letting the air in his lungs bear him the last few feet upward until he, too, was above the surface. The boat was only fifty feet away, and that meant safety. But when he looked back, he saw the blue shark, much closer, heading straight for them.

Kara's voice hit his ears. "Move slowly!"

He obeyed, stretching his body out clumsily until most of it was horizontal, watching the stiff fin and the shadowy bulk under it not more than five feet away.

Kara reached for her face mask, tearing it from her head. Then, as the shark came beside her, she threw it at him. It hit the top of his long snout and slipped away, sinking. Eric caught his breath as the jaws opened and he saw jagged rows of sharp teeth for one awful moment before it dived after the mask and disappeared.

Kara moved quickly now, swimming toward the boat with powerful strokes, and Tom and Eric churned through the water after her. When they had reached it safely and were back on board, Eric could only sink thankfully into the nearest seat.

Kara seemed composed, and angry. "You two shouldn't have come after me. I told you I'd be all right. You should have stayed right here on the boat."

Tom looked at her wearily, his face mask dangling from one limp hand. "Mom, we couldn't stay here when you were in danger. What made you go down there with those sharks?"

She shook her head stubbornly. "I wasn't in any danger."

"They could have killed you."

"They only kill for food, when they're hungry. Just like any other fish. Just like wild animals."

Tom didn't seem convinced. "But you stayed under even though your air was nearly gone. You must have known it was. I couldn't just wait here for you."

Kara didn't argue further. She stripped off her diving gear and then, while Tom and Eric did the same, she brought three glasses of orange juice from the cabin.

While they sat on the sunny deck and drank, and watched the birds on the rocky island nearby, Eric tried to make cheerful small talk. It was no use. They were all too disturbed by what had happened. It was only during the boat ride back to the marina that they had all relaxed enough to talk about other things. Then Tom drove Eric back to his uncle's in the convertible.

They didn't discuss the day's strange event as they drove. It was on both of their minds, Eric knew, but it was too fresh and too bewildering, and so they talked about surfing and school and girls, and soon Tom was pulling the convertible to the curb in front of Uncle Walter's house.

"Remember we're going to talk to Al tomorrow," he said. "Okay if I pick you up about nine?"

"Sure. See you." Eric waved and went slowly up the flagstone walk. The house was cool and quiet as he entered. He looked around for his uncle, but the rooms were empty. It was when he went to the kitchen for a snack that he found the note, held by a magnet to the refrigerator door. He recognized his uncle's distinctive scrawl that filled the whole page. "Eric, something unexpected came up and I have to go out. Might not be back until late tonight. Lots of food in fridge."

Eric made himself a lunch of cold chicken, salad, and ice cream, and tried to forget the haunting image, in his mind, of Kara swimming among those big blue sharks. He wished his uncle were there so they could talk it over, maybe make some sense out of it.

After lunch he went exploring by himself along La Jolla's beaches and rocky coves. When he returned home, the phone was ringing. It was his uncle, telling him that some of the scientists from Scripps had been called to Santa Barbara, himself included. They were investigating a strange yellow stream of unknown origin running along the coast, and wouldn't return for a day or two. Disappointed, Eric made himself a light dinner and found a book about sharks in his uncle's library. But although he was interested in learning more about them, the full-color pictures in the book made him uneasy, reminding him of the day's events. He decided to phone home, then go to bed early. It had been an exciting day, after all.

Next morning, as Tom and Eric drove toward the marina to meet Al Madow, Tom finally brought up the subject of his mother. He spoke hesitantly. "That was some big deal yesterday, huh? I mean my mom and those sharks."

"Yeah," Eric agreed. "I've never seen anything like it."

"Well—uh—what did you think?"

"About your mom? I think she sure likes sharks."

"Yeah. That's what I thought." Tom gazed thoughtfully at the road ahead. "But when I asked her yesterday, after we got home, how come she wasn't afraid of them—she just told me I wouldn't understand, almost like she didn't want to talk about it again."

"I don't understand either. If she liked porpoises or seals, that would make more sense. But *sharks?*"

"She says she's been swimming with them before like that."

"You've got to be kidding!" Eric glanced at Tom's face and saw fear there, like his own, that drew his face tight and ringed his eyes with dark shadows. "Well," Eric said lamely, "maybe we can talk her out of doing it any more."

"Yeah. I hope so."

"I've read about a married couple, the Taylors, who photograph sharks all the time. They practically live in the water with them, and they do just fine."

"The sharks?"

"No, the Taylors."

Tom nodded, but the information didn't seem to cheer him.

Eric decided the subject should be dropped. "This Al Madow we're going to see—is he partners with your mother in the marina?"

"No. He was my dad's partner. Mom and I just own shares in it now. Al bought out most of it and he runs the place. He said he wanted to be sure Mom and I were taken care of, so he arranged for us to keep part of it when Dad disappeared. Al's been almost like a father to me all my life, and he's really good to Mom, too." Tom turned the MG onto the side street leading to the marina. "Only thing is, Mom doesn't let him come around much. She doesn't care much about friends."

"Doesn't she get lonely when you're at school?"

"Guess not," Tom shrugged. "She never says so."

The more Eric learned about Kara Kelsey, the less he liked her. Here was Al Madow, taking good care of her, and she didn't even want to be friendly with him, just as she stayed aloof from Uncle Walter and the others at the university. Al yesterday seemed like a really nice

42

guy, he thought. "But what are we going to ask him?" he wondered out loud.

"Al? I guess we can just ask him to tell us all he knows about my dad." Tom pulled the car into a space beside a blue Mustang.

"Won't he wonder why we're asking?"

"I don't think he'll get the idea we're investigating if we just talk about Dad. But I guess I should do most of the talking."

"Sure. And by the way," Eric said as they headed down the slope, "I called my father last night. He couldn't give me any more information. Said he really didn't know your dad all that well."

"Okay. Thanks anyway."

They went along the path between the two buildings. A mist hung over the ocean this morning, chilling the air and shrouding the sun. A tall steel crane stood in front of the warehouse, its base festooned with brown seaweed, its cables drooping on the pavement. Inside the shed, a wooden-hulled sailing ship rested on supports and a man with a wrestler's body, clad in blue overalls, was pulling damaged wood from its splintered side, whistling as he worked.

"Good morning, Al," Tom called to him.

Al Madow turned to them, stripping off one of his work gloves, swiping the back of his hand across his shiny forehead. Eric could see that this man might once have been handsome. His smile softened the lines that the sun and salty winds had etched into his face, and his hand covered his receding hairline. "Well, here you are, my two helpers, right on time," he said.

"No fishing today?" Tom asked him.

"Can't today. Here's this seafarer in distress, needing prompt attention, with a hole in her side big enough to drop her engine through." He patted the broken wood affectionately. "But I'll tell you what. If you two would take on some barnacle scraping for me, I'll buy you each a big steak for lunch. How about it?"

Tom looked at Eric. "Want to?"

"I've never done it before. How do you scrape barnacles?"

"We just get into our scuba gear and take some scrapers with us. Then we dive under the boat and go to work." Tom turned to Al. "Which one needs the scraping?"

"That forty-foot yacht over there. The owner asked me to find somebody. Thought you might want the job. Shouldn't take more than a couple hours, with no sweat."

"I can give it a try," Eric said. "But I took my swim fins home with me yesterday."

"That's okay," Al said. "The rest of your gear is still stowed on the *Remora,* isn't it, Tom? I think we can dig up a pair of flippers around here to fit you, Eric."

The yacht was anchored at the end of a jetty—looming tall and trim, her white hull shining. Beyond her, out in the channel, another boat chugged into the marina, loud talk and laughter coming from its deck. The strong odor of dead fish made Eric's nose wrinkle. "Smells like a fishing boat," he said.

Tom peered through the mist. "Must be the *Jolly Jack.* That's Captain Jack's ship. He's been taking passengers out deep-sea fishing again. He cleans their catch right on board and dumps the leavings anywhere he feels like it." He pointed down to the water beside the jetty. "Look at that."

A fishhead floated by on a rippling wave, followed by a bobbing beer can.

"Even though it's fish, it's foul," Eric remarked.

Tom groaned. "So's that joke. Anyway, I'm pretty sure Al's warned him before about this, but he's done things the same way for years. He's not about to change."

They dove off the jetty. As they went under the hull of the yacht, Eric noticed how murky the water was, even less than ten feet below the surface. Yesterday, deep in the kelp bed, visibility had been better. He felt ashamed that his fellow man could be responsible for such pollution, dirtying the ocean with substances far more toxic and dangerous than fishheads and beer cans.

The underside of the ship was encrusted with a thick layer of purplish-blue shells entwined in clumps of seaweed. Tom demonstrated how to scrape them off, sliding his scraper under the clumps and lifting, so that a patch of barnacles fell off at every swipe. When Eric mastered the motions, he went to the stern of the boat and worked his way toward Tom.

After a while he became absorbed in the work, lulled by the mechanical motions of scraping and lifting, and the sound of his own breathing—the hollow rasp as he inhaled and the bubbling as he breathed out. In this gray, silent world he seemed completely alone, suspended in space and time like an astronaut in a capsule.

Then something bumped against his outstretched legs. Annoyed, he moved his legs under him and turned his head to see what it was. Tentacles spread and then came together before they disappeared in the turgid water. It must have been a squid, passing in a hurry. A good-sized one, too. Eric looked around to see if there were others.

And then he saw the eye. It *was* an eye, set in a grayish-brown head, but it had no pupil. It looked like a round black hole. He stared, and turned cold as the fish moved silently past him. He saw the gleam of its white underside and the rippling of its gill slits and then, as his gaze went upward, he saw the rigid dorsal fin. Shock numbed him so that his fingers could no longer hold the scraper and it dropped away while he watched the shark's tail disappear in the gloom a few feet away.

Now he jerked into motion, clawing the barncles down the length of the ship, thrusting his fins to help speed him onward. Tom's figure was a blur in the soupy water. Eric clutched at his arm for a fraction of a second to warn him, then he flashed past, swimming upward. It wasn't a long way to the surface. By the time Tom's head appeared, Eric was yanking himself up onto the jetty.

Tom looked at him curiously through his face mask while he pulled his mouthpiece from between his teeth. "What's the matter?"

"Shark," Eric panted. "Shark down there."

Tom looked anxiously into the water and then swiftly pulled himself onto the dock. "Are you sure?"

"Yeah."

"A big one?"

Eric nodded.

Tom frowned in the direction of the channel. "All those fish scraps must have attracted it. Probably followed the fishing boat in from the open sea. How big was it?"

"I don't know." Eric took in deep breaths, all the time scanning the water. "It wasn't as big as those blues we saw yesterday. It was probably six or seven feet."

"What kind was it, do you know?"

Eric stared silently at the rippling water of the channel.

"A hornshark?" Tom went on. "A sand tiger? They're harmless. Nothing to get excited about."

"This wasn't harmless."

Tom stared at him.

"It's really weird!" Eric rubbed the back of his neck, where gooseflesh was prickling. "I've never even seen a live shark in the ocean before this summer, and in the last two days I've dived among four of them. But that one I saw down there . . ."

"What was it?"

"I know what I *think* it was. I think it was a great white shark."

4 • The Watchers

"A great white shark?" Tom's freckles looked darker as he paled. He jerked his head to look out past the line of boats to the open sea.

Eric stared out there, too, but saw no fin jutting through the ripples of the channel. The water seemed ominously calm. He took off his flippers and stood up. "We'd better tell Al."

They ran along the jetty so fast that they were both out of breath when they reached the warehouse.

Al saw them coming. "What's up? You two see a ghost?"

"A great white shark!" Eric told his story, describing the shark as exactly as he could. Then Tom told about the fishing boat, and how they'd seen fish scraps floating in the marina.

Al's sunburned face looked grave. "Are you sure you know what a great white looks like?"

"I think so," Eric said. "I was reading about sharks

last night. The book had pictures. The shark I saw had the same sort of cone-shaped head and the same eyes."

Al peeled off his gloves and tossed them on the ground. "Okay. You'd better show me."

They hurried toward the slip where Eric and Tom had been working. They passed a man in shorts who was painting his sailboat, and Al called him. "Hey, Jim!"

Jim poked his head around the corner of the cabin to see who was calling. "Hi, Al."

"You seen any sharks around the marina?"

"No. Why?"

Al paused in front of the sailboat. "These boys were scraping the *Lucky Lucy* down there," he pointed to the end of the jetty. "Eric saw a shark. Looked like it might be a great white."

Jim whistled, long and low, pushing his sailor cap to the back of his head. "A great white? Around *here?*" He came to the bow of the boat and looked down at them. "Better send out warnings, Al."

Al looked around at the empty boats. "Lucky there aren't many people out here today, but if you see any, give them the word. We're going to take a look now."

"Wait for me!" Jim jumped down and hurried after them.

When they reached the yacht, Al studied the waters beside it. Then, seeing nothing, he climbed on board the *Lucky Lucy,* with the others close behind. As they went to the stern, Jim questioned Eric about what he'd seen.

When Eric had told him, he whistled again. "Sounds like the white death, all right. Man! Just like in 'Jaws'!"

They all hung over the rail and looked into the murky water below them.

"Can't see anything looks like a shark," Al said finally, "but the water's all mucked up with garbage. Anybody see anything?"

Eric looked hard into the cloudy depths, remembering the shadowy shape and the fathomless black eye. What if he'd been mistaken? It would be embarrassing to cause all this fuss for nothing. "Can't see anything now, but I'm sure I saw it before," he said. "I know I did."

"Better warn everyone, even if you are mistaken," Jim said. "A mistake can't hurt, but a white shark sure can."

"I'll report it to the Coast Guard," Al said. "They have a shark watch. Helicopters. If there's a great white or any other big shark around, they'll spot it."

Jim went with them as far as his sailboat. "I'll keep an eye out," he said, and the others headed back to Al's office.

While Al phoned the Coast Guard, Eric and Tom dressed in the bathroom, changing their bathing suits for jeans and T-shirts. When they came out again, Al looked more cheerful.

"They'll have a helicopter out right away. In the meantime, all we can do is wait. You boys feel like eating those steaks I promised you?"

"I'd like to stay here and see if they find the shark," Eric said.

"We'll just go to the *Gull's Nest,* right over there." He pointed to the restaurant across from the warehouse. "It's got a good view of the channel. If any news comes, we'll have it right away."

The *Gull's Nest* was cool and dim, and nearly empty.

Once they were seated in a booth next to the wide windows, Eric began to relax. The smell of steak came from the kitchen, and when Al suggested items from the large menu, Eric realized how hungry he was.

At first they could only talk about the shark. Eric had to go over and over the description, and Al told them stories of sharks he'd seen and heard about, and described how he had once caught a mako off Catalina Island several years ago. But neither Tom nor Eric mentioned their meeting with the big blue sharks the day before, almost as though it were a shameful secret. Eric understood. Tom didn't want to mention Kara's incredible behavior. He didn't blame Tom.

While they ate their steaks, Tom brought up the subject of his father, and Eric remembered that was the reason they'd come here today.

"You knew Dad pretty well, didn't you, Al?"

"Well sure I did. We were partners here for nearly three years, and good friends a couple years before that."

"Did he ever work on the boats, like you do?"

Al shook his head, thin wisps of his graying hair swaying slightly. "That was mostly my job. Steve liked to tinker with things."

"What kind of things?"

"All kinds of things. Motors. He was partial to mechanical things." Al's eyes narrowed slightly as he looked at Tom. "Why?"

"I don't know anything much about him, Al. I never knew him. And I guess—I guess a guy ought to know something about his own father."

"Oh, sure." Al's voice softened. "Sure. I understand. Well, what can I tell you? He was smart. Full of vim and vigor. And he'd get all wound up on some subjects. All enthusiastic. He'd bend my ear about some new project nearly every time we were together. Ask your mother about that.''

"I've asked her about Dad," Tom said quietly.

"And doesn't she say the same thing?" The question sounded casual, but Eric caught the expression on Al's face—the expression he couldn't know was showing— and knew that what he asked wasn't casual at all. Al wanted very much to know what Kara had told Tom about his father.

"She—she didn't say that, exactly." Tom was getting that tight, strained look again.

"What does she say about him?" Curiosity was naked on Al's face now, but Eric was the only one who saw it. Tom was staring out the window with hurt eyes.

"What is it, son?" Al urged him.

"She doesn't talk much about him. All she says is . . ."

"Yes?"

"Well . . . she says he was weak. Because he took off with some other woman that night.''

Eric felt surprise and sympathy for Tom. Now he understood why his friend had been reluctant to explain this before.

"That's what she said happened." Tom looked at Al, now, words pouring out of him in a wavering stream. "That he just deserted her and me, because he had some other woman. And he never came back because he didn't want to.''

The tension seemed to leave Al. He leaned back in

52

his chair. "It's a hard thing to know, son, but maybe that's true. Maybe you ought to face facts."

"What facts?" Tom looked angry. "Mom said she never saw any other woman—never knew there was one before that night. How does she know?"

"Maybe there were signs."

"I've asked her, but she doesn't say anything except that he was weak. Al, you knew him. Was he weak? Is it true that's why he left us?"

The big man glanced around. Two men had come in and were taking seats at the far end of the room, but Al lowered his voice as though worried that they might hear. "Now, now, son. Let's not get all bent out of shape. I don't know if it's true or not. Nobody knows for sure at this point. But your mother must know him. She was married to him, after all. Now take a bite or two out of your steak before it gets cold."

Tom gazed out the window again, where the mist had lifted and a helicopter could be seen flying low over the marina. Sunlight struck blinding flashes of silver off the water. "Mom never talks about him at all, except to say things like that. But he must have been okay. He was in the Marine Corps once. I know because some of his old stuff is in his den—pictures and ribbons and things. And he went to college and worked hard, and earned the money to buy half the marina and pay for our house."

In the pause that followed, Eric spoke. "My father knew him slightly. He says Stephen Kelsey was very important among environmentalists."

Al had been cutting his steak, but now his head snapped up and he looked curiously at Eric. "Who's your dad?"

"Doctor Randall Thorne."

"Can't say as I've ever heard of him."

"He's a Professor of Agronomy at Midwest University. He's involved in conservationist work quite a bit, and he knows most of the people who are." Eric didn't mention his father's connection with the International Agricultural Foundation. Tom was trying to find out about *his* father, after all, and it seemed that Al was the one asking most of the questions. "Did you know anything about Steve Kelsey's work with conservation?" he asked.

"Nothing like that," Al said flatly. "Conservation? No, nothing like that."

"Or any inventions of his?" Eric hoped he wasn't saying too much, but it was obvious that Tom was upset, and his questions hadn't done anything much except upset him further.

"Steve invented something?" Now Al seemed amazed. "What?"

But Eric wasn't going to answer questions. He was going to ask them "Didn't you know about any of his inventions? You two were partners in a business. It seems strange you wouldn't know."

Al was irritated at this. His tone had a rough edge. "I'll tell you something I've not told many people. It doesn't matter now. It's been sixteen years, after all. Steve and I were partners, sure, but we were poles apart. A matter of personalities."

Tom stared at him. "Al, I always thought . . ."

"Oh, we didn't quarrel . . . didn't air our differences, Son. Especially not so Kara would notice. No, we ran the business together, but Steve did his thing and I did mine. We both knew we had to make a go of the marina. And we both cared too much for Kara . . ." Al was looking beyond them now, into the past, his voice softening. "We were a lot closer then in some ways, Son. At first, that is. Three musketeers, we were, Steve and Kara and me."

Tom glanced at Eric with a look that said he didn't understand all this, and Al, returning suddenly to the present, caught the glance. His face reddened slightly and one hand waved as though trying to brush his words away. "Friends, that is. Just good friends. But do you know that Steve got some crazy idea I was trying to get *too* friendly with Kara." he smiled to illustrate just how ridiculous that idea was, looking from one to the other with curling lips and raised eyebrows.

Eric was embarrassed. Tom must have felt the same way, for he spoke a little too quickly. "Do you have any idea, Al, what happened to Dad that night he disappeared?"

"No, Son, I don't, and that's the truth." Al busied himself with his steak. "I didn't see him at all that day, though I did see the *Kelpie* moored right in her usual place. He must have taken her out while I was busy somewhere else. I told all this to the police at the time."

"The *Kelpie* was the boat he was on that night?" Tom asked.

Al nodded, chewing steak, staring thoughtfully at him. "So you're bound and determined to find out what happened to Steve, are you?"

"Oh, no." Tom's tone was indifferent. "Not really. I just want to find out all I can about Dad, like I told you. And I can't help wondering . . ."

"Well, as the French say, you might *cherchez la femme*. If Kara says there was a woman in the picture, then I'd take her word for it."

The waitress came with the bill, and after he'd paid for their lunch, Al spoke briskly. "We'd better go find out about that shark."

They walked back to his office, noting the Coast Guard helicopter still flying over the channel, and Al sat down behind his desk. But after he'd phoned the authorities, he hung up, shaking his head. "They don't see sharks in the water. None at all."

Eric looked out the window. The day was clear, but he remembered the murky ocean. "That water is as cloudy as pea soup. How could they tell?"

"If they don't see a shark, there's nothing they can do." Al shrugged his heavy shoulders. "But if you boys would like to stay around and help out for the rest of the day, I'm up to my eyebrows in work. I could sure use a couple of good hands at—say—five bucks an hour."

"Guess not," Tom said. "There's a few things we were going to do this afternoon. But thanks a lot for the lunch."

"You both earned it," Al said.

When they were walking up the slope toward the parking lot, Eric voiced his frustration. "I know I saw a shark down there. What happens if somebody gets hurt?"

Tom seemed preoccupied. "I don't know. I don't know what else we could do about the shark. But I *do* know that I didn't like what Al told me. All that stuff about my mom and dad." He opened the door of the MG and got in.

56

Eric sat down on the other side. "Do you think he was telling all he knows?"

"I'm not sure, but I'm beginning to wonder about him. I always thought he and my dad were best friends. Now I guess I can understand why Mom doesn't let him hang around our house. He seems to have a big thing going for her, no matter what he says. I used to think he was just being really nice to us."

"Yeah," Eric said. "I can't really imagine your mom getting romantic over him."

"I can't see Mom getting romantic, period. She's not like that." Tom started the car and backed out of the parking space. "One thing's for sure, though. I guess I really tipped off to Al that we're investigating Dad's disappearance."

They drove through the gate and along the short street, but just before they reached the corner, Tom pulled the car to the curb.

"What's the matter?" Eric asked.

"I've got to fasten my seat belt. Better do yours, too. This car doesn't have a roll bar, and Mom gets upset about my driving with the top down and no seat belt."

Eric fastened the strap, then glanced in the sideview mirror. It had been jarred out of position, and he could see the reflection of the parking lot they had just left. "Hey! There's Al now, getting into that blue Mustang."

Tom turned around to look. "I wonder where he's going? He said he was up to his eyebrows in work."

"That *is* strange. Why didn't he walk up to the parking lot with us?"

They looked at each other, wondering.

"Think he doesn't want us to know that he's going

57

somewhere?'' Eric moved the mirror so he could keep Al in view.

"Sure seems that way, doesn't it?''

"Yeah. And it must be something important if he's going to leave the marina with the threat of a shark in the water, besides all that work.''

Tom gave Eric a wicked look. "Should we tag along behind him and see where he's heading?''

"It couldn't hurt. But we'd better get out of his sight before he drives up this way.''

Eric looked around. They were stopped in the shelter of spreading eucalyptus branches. Next to them was the driveway of a house. "If we back in there he won't be likely to see us through all these leaves.''

Tom nodded, and backed the car into the driveway. Then they waited, half hidden in the shade of the overhanging tree, and watched for Al Madow to pass.

5 • Chase

In a moment the blue Mustang sped past them, going so fast that Al Madow, inside the car, was only a blur.

"Wait till he turns the corner. We don't want him to see us," Eric said.

"Okay, but we don't want to lose him." Tom kept the motor of the MG purring, then inched out onto the street. The Mustang was gone. They sped to the corner, and looked both ways.

"There!" Eric pointed to the right, where a blue car had stopped for a red signal. "But there's only a couple of other cars on the road. He'll see us. Better wait here a minute."

Tom waited at the corner, watching as the light turned green and the Mustang drove away. As it crossed the intersection, a brown van came from a side street and turned right, closing in behind Al's car. Tom turned the corner and drove the MG after the brown van, sighing with relief as they made the green light, following as close to the van as they could to keep out of Al's vision. The traffic was still thin, and when the van pulled into the left lane to make a turn, the Mustang was less than a block away from them, with no cars between to hide them.

Tom turned the corner.

"What are you doing?" Eric craned his neck, trying to see the Mustang. "We're going to lose him."

"I think he saw us. He must have."

"He probably wasn't looking in his rearview mirror," Eric said confidently. "He's traveling fast so he's probably got his eyes glued to the road."

"You think so?" Tom pulled the car back into the traffic lane. "I'll have to go around the next corner now."

"Hurry!"

Tom made a left turn at the next street and went around the block to get back on La Jolla Boulevard, but as he turned right he frowned. "I don't see him."

Eric scanned the road ahead and then, just to be sure, turned to look behind them. There was no blue Mustang in sight. "Keep on going straight. Maybe we can still catch up with him."

They drove several more blocks without sighting Al, and were just about ready to give up the search when Eric gave a shout and pointed. Far ahead was a glimmer of dark blue turning right. "There he is!"

"You sure it's him?" Tom asked doubtfully.

"Pretty sure."

They waited impatiently behind several cars at the next stoplight, then had to proceed slowly behind a bus for another quarter mile until they could turn the same corner.

"We've lost him again." Tom looked down the empty street.

"We seem to be heading for Mission Bay. Let's just go on."

"I never knew how hard it was to tail somebody!" Tom pushed a strand of sandy hair off his sweating forehead. "Now I wonder how they do it on all those TV shows."

They could see the bay ahead of them, but there was no sign of the blue Mustang.

"Well," Tom said finally, "there isn't much use looking any more. He could be anywhere. Let's go back to my house. I've got an idea. I want to go through Dad's den."

"Think we can find something there?"

Tom turned a corner. "Maybe. We don't have much to go on now. I should have asked Al if he knew any of Dad's other friends."

"I have a feeling he wouldn't have told you if he—" Eric broke off as they passed a side street. "It was there! The Mustang!"

"I didn't see it. Where was it?"

"Parked near the bay. Go around this block and back up that last street."

"What if he sees us?"

"I think the car was empty. Anyway, we have to take that chance, don't we? Otherwise how will we find out what he's doing here?"

As soon as they had gone around the block, they saw Al's car. It was parked near a grassy slope, where they could see children playing, and beyond, in the bay, people on various kinds of watercraft were skimming on the bright water. As Tom drove slowly toward the car, he and Eric scanned the crowd, looking for Al.

A Datsun ahead of them stopped to let pedestrians cross. Eric glanced to his right. There was Al, standing under a tree, talking to another man.

Tom saw them at the same time. "There's nowhere to hide," he groaned, and just as he spoke, Al looked up and saw them. His ruddy face turned deeper red, and for a moment Eric thought he saw anger there before Al forced a smile.

"Rats!" Tom put on a smile, and Eric waved, feeling uncomfortable.

The man with Al saw them, too, but now he turned away and ambled toward the bay. If he was trying to hide his face from them, Eric thought, it was too late. He'd already taken a good look. It was a remarkable face, thin and rather pointed, with very dark eyes and thick, bushy dark eyebrows that met over his nose.

The Datsun moved forward. Tom let out a long, relieved breath and jolted the car into motion, passing Al.

"Great spies we'd make!"

"Well, we're good detectives," Eric said. "We caught Al in the act."

"What act? Maybe he was only rapping about nothing much with a stranger."

"If that's the case, then he came a long way to do it, in an awful hurry."

"Yeah—they did look pretty deep in conversation, before they saw us."

"You ever seen that other guy before?" Eric asked.

"No. I don't know who he is."

Eric rubbed his ear thoughtfully. "The only reason I

can think of why Al would meet him here is that they didn't want anyone to see them together, or hear what they were saying."

"So they meet in a public park?" Tom looked skeptical. "Everyone could see them, right out in the open like that."

"But not people either of them knew. If that man came to the marina, or Al went to his place, they'd be seen by someone they knew. Here, all these people would most likely be strangers who wouldn't even notice them." The more Eric thought about it, the more logical it seemed.

"So why would they meet here to talk? Why not do it over the phone? Why did Al have to come all the way out here?"

"Well, maybe it was so important that he was afraid to use the phone. Other people might be around to hear, or maybe Al or that other guy worry about their phones being tapped."

Tom sent him a sidelong glance. "Come on! Phone tapping? Sounds like dumb secret agent stuff."

"Hey, your dad disappeared, and you said yourself that he might have been killed. That's not dumb secret agent stuff."

"You mean you think Al might have had something to do with that?"

"Don't you?" Eric was surprised. "That's why we followed him, isn't it? I mean, you were asking him questions about your Dad's disappearance, and five minutes later he's acting very suspiciously."

"I guess you're right. I guess I do suspect Al. It's just that he's always been a great guy. Almost like a father." He looked toward Eric, his eyes bewildered. "We're not just playing kid's games, are we?"

Realization hit Eric. This search didn't mean as much to him as it did to Tom and here he'd been stomping all over Tom's feelings without even thinking about it. He'd have to remember that Kara and Al were the only family Tom had left. He'd have to try to put himself in Tom's place. But after all, it had been Tom's idea. "Are you sure you want to go ahead with this?" he asked seriously. "Maybe we should just forget the investigation."

"No!" Tom's voice was sharp and positive. "I've thought about it a whole lot, and I'm sure. I want to know the truth, even if it hurts."

"Okay." Once again Eric thought Tom was a pretty brave guy. But he couldn't help wondering how he would feel if Kara turned out to be the guilty one.

Tom's voice broke into these thoughts. "Come on, let's try to figure this out. What if Al and that guy did have something to do with Dad's disappearance? Al catches onto the fact that we're trying to find out about it, and he gets worried about what we might discover, so he tells this guy to watch out for us."

"Right. And he's in a hurry to warn him, in case we find out something pretty quick." Eric's thoughts raced as he tried to put the few pieces of this puzzle together to make some sort of logical picture. "If this other guy's a criminal, then Al wouldn't want anyone to know they're connected. So he doesn't phone him or meet him anywhere they could be recognized."

"Sure. A phone call would show up on his phone bill, so it would be a record showing they knew each other."

64

As the boat stopped, the speedboat drew up beside them again, and its occupant produced a dockline. After a couple of tries, while both boats tossed on the waves, he managed to secure his vessel to the *Remora*. Then he climbed aboard.

He was dressed in exactly the same way as his companion, but instead of a gun, this man carried a hatchet. He went up to the first man and said something Eric couldn't hear.

While their two captors were talking, Tom moved swiftly. He reached toward his radiotelephone and pressed the transmission switch. He couldn't send a message without being heard by the two men on board, but Eric knew what he was doing. Someone would be at a receiver. Someone would hear what was going on. Someone *had* to be listening! Because he was pretty sure these men had brought them out here, miles from the coast, to kill them, and there seemed nothing they could do to stop them. He kept his eyes on them, fear tensing his body and sharpening his senses.

The man carrying the hatchet looked toward them. Eric suddenly realized he could see the light on the radiotelephone. He moved his body to hide it, but it was too late. The man came at them, shoved Eric aside, and with two forceful swings of his weapon demolished their only hope of rescue.

Furious, Eric lashed out with his hands, grabbing at the swinging arm to stop it from chopping again. As he did so, the man jerked his arm powerfully, freeing it. He turned his plastic face toward Eric. The last rays of the sun fell on it, turning it a blinding golden-black, impenetrable and unreadable; an inhuman mask where a human face should be. And the thing behind it lifted its arm to swing the hatchet down on Eric's head.

"Jess! No!" The other man raced toward him. "Not like that!" He threw himself against his friend, knocking him off balance so that the blade of the hatchet hit the control console.

Eric, shivering, dodged away, his forehead beading with sweat. The man called Jess lashed out at the other man with an angry shove, and the gun he held dropped on the deck. Tom swooped down and picked it up. He leveled it at the two men. "Okay, step back both of you! Back toward the stern."

The two dark visors snapped toward him, but neither man moved. Jess still held his hatchet. Eric moved to take it from him, but it felt as though it were welded to Jess's fist.

"No you don't," Jess growled, the threat in his tone unmistakable.

"Give him the hatchet!" Tom ordered, but his voice broke on the words, his nervousness betrayed.

Eric spoke quickly, gruffly, to try to cover for him. "Give it to me."

"I'll give it to you in the neck if you try to touch it!"

"I'll shoot. I swear I will." Tom stepped back a pace. "Now give him that hatchet. Give it over by the handle, nice and easy."

Eric reached out to receive it, pretending a confidence he didn't feel. Tom looked too nervous, too unsure of himself, and the gun was shaking in his trembling hand. But if he could get that hatchet, then both of them would have weapons.

Jess only shook his head. "Go ahead. Shoot."

82

Tom's face was white. He lifted his hand slowly. The gun wavered as it rose.

And one of the men laughed.

The laugh was cut short as the gun went off with a terrible *crack!* as though the world itself were breaking in two. Then there was silence. The helmeted men stood rigidly for a moment, then looked to see who had been hit. But the shot had gone wild.

Tom was the first to realize it. Anger and fear gave him a ferocious expression; his hand was steady and his voice strong. "That shot was only a warning. The next one won't be. Now step back, both of you." He flourished the gun as though he were comfortable with it at last.

The two faceless men backed away.

Eric watched. Should he try again to get that hatchet, or should he let Tom handle things? In the split second he was wondering this, Tom took the initiative. "You—drop the hatchet on the deck. Fast!"

The weapon clanged against the metal engine hatch and clunked to the floor.

"Now take off those helmets." Tom's skin glimmered palely in the fading light as he walked away from the steering house to get a better look at the faces that would soon be revealed, but as he moved, a high wave slapped against the *Remora's* port. The cruiser lurched. Tom lost his footing and fell. The gun jolted out of his hand and skidded toward the two men.

Eric made a dive for it, but too late. Jess was on his knees in front of him, hatchet in one hand, gun in the other. He rose with a triumphant laugh, and handed the gun to his companion. "Game's over, guys," he said.

"Time for the real thing. Now stand there by the railing with your hands up, right there where I can watch you." He waited until his orders had been obeyed, then turned to the other man. "Let's get going. It's nearly dark now."

The faceless helmet moved up and down in agreement. "You start with the electrical system. I'll take care of the engines."

Tom and Eric watched them helplessly as they wrecked the *Remora*. One of them took the distributor cap from the engine and tossed it overboard. The other smashed the lights, then went to the console to chop at the steering equipment. They destroyed the life raft and threw life vests and batteries over the side.

Eric felt numb. Would the men kill him and Tom, or just leave them adrift? He prayed silently. The image of his family rose in his mind. If he was going to die, he at least wanted to know the reason for it. He didn't know these men, and Tom didn't seem to, either. Why were they destroying the *Remora?* What connection did they have with anything or anyone?

The two men finished their terrible task quickly, then turned to Eric and Tom. Eric steeled himself for what might come.

The man with the gun spoke. "Stay nice and quiet until we're gone, and we won't hurt you this time. But if you two live through this, you better remember something and remember it good: There better not be a next time." He moved to the railing where the speedboat was tied, motioning for his companion to board it while he held the gun pointed at them. "You be good boys. Stay home. Don't try to play detective any more."

Curiosity made Eric bold. "What's that supposed to mean?"

"Just what I said."

"But what are you talking about? We're not detectives." Eric tried to sound really mystified, but it wasn't all acting. Was this man telling them to stop investigating Steve Kelsey's disappearance?

"Look, kid . . ." the voice was exasperated.

"But if you're warning us, tell us what you're warning us about."

"Hey, come on!" the other man called from the speedboat. "Gossip some other time. We got to get out of here."

"Okay." The gunman climbed over the rail and into the speedboat, but he spoke as he untied the dock line that held it. "Stay away from the Indian!" Then the motor roared and the boat moved away leaving Eric and Tom to stare after it.

"Indian?" Eric said finally. "He must mean Ben Brightstar."

Tom was more worried about the boat. "Those rotten, no-good turkeys! Look what they did!" He swept his hand despondently around.

"At least we're alive. I thought for a minute . . ."

Tom grinned suddenly. "Anyway, we gave them a hard time for a while, didn't we?"

"When you got their gun? We sure did!"

"When I fired that thing, I thought they were going to start begging for mercy." Tom's face grew sad again. "If I'd been able to hold on to that gun, none of this would have happened." He went to the steering house and surveyed the broken remains.

Eric looked at the heaving ocean. It was getting dark, and a mist was beginning to shroud their boat. It was an eerie feeling, riding silently on the swell, knowing they couldn't start the motors and go home. "I wonder if the Coast Guard will find us?"

"How can they? I couldn't give them our position. We don't have any lights, and they threw out all our flares."

"But they'll know we're missing. They'll be looking for us."

Tom came up beside him and leaned wearily on the railing. "Mom and your uncle are in Santa Barbara, remember? When they phone and we're not there they'll just think we're out somewhere, at a movie or something." He shook his head. "No. Nobody's going to be looking for us. Not tonight. And even if they were, they might never see us."

Eric suddenly remembered. "Al! He knows we took the boat out." But then a thought occurred to him, and he knew it must have come to Tom, too.

"Yeah." Tom put the thought into words. "Al was the only one who knew we took the boat out, so maybe he sent those two men after us."

"Otherwise, how would anyone know we were going to see Ben Brightstar," Eric finished. "But you didn't tell Al who you were going to see. You just said it was someone who knew your dad."

"Right. But if Al sent those men to find us, they could have just followed us and figured out where we were going."

"And if that's the case," Eric said, "he won't be reporting us missing."

86

Silence fell between them for a moment until Eric said, "Tom, there was someone else who knew where we were going. Ben Brightstar knew."

"You think he might have sent those men to warn us off? But why? All he had to do was refuse to see me. Or he could have said he didn't know anything about Dad."

Eric shrugged. "It doesn't make any sense. None of it does." He stared out across the misty water, hoping that Tom was wrong—hoping that somehow, someone would know they were missing and would be searching for them. But the ocean was very big, and the boat was very small.

For the first time, he realized that they might be here for days. Sooner or later, someone would see them. But how long could they survive?

7 ● *Monster From the Deep*

Night was closing in on them. There was no moon, or at least none they could see through the mist. Eric and Tom sat in the wreckage of the *Remora*, wondering what to do now.

"Those creeps ruined everything we could use," Tom said angrily. "Everything's smashed, torn out, destroyed. And we don't even know where we are."

"We must be at least twenty miles from the shore," Eric said.

"They wrecked all the instruments. There's no way to tell."

Eric felt despondent. They were way off the path of the many boats that sailed the coastline. He wasn't sure how far the Coast Guard patrolled. And here they were alone on the vast sea, in the darkness, with no way to get help. As if this wasn't enough, another thought struck him. "What if that gunshot made a hole in the hull?"

"When that creep shot at the deck? Rats! I'd forgotten about that."

Eric was sorry he'd mentioned it. "We can't do anything about it in the dark, anyway. Let's forget it."

"It would have had to have enough force to go through the deck of the steering house and the cabin floor, too. But I don't know." Tom's voice was almost a wail. "If we could only do something."

"Yeah." Anything would be better than sitting here, feeling sorry for themselves. "What about dropping anchor? Should we do that, so we don't drift?"

Tom thought it over. "There's a chance we could drift into some rocks, all right, but we might drift further toward shore instead."

"Well, we couldn't be worse off, even if we did hit rocks. Not unless we hit them hard enough to sink the ship, and that isn't likely in this weather."

"Let's just let her drift. The closer to shore we can get, the more chance we have of being found."

"Right," Eric said without conviction. "They'll find us, all right. Somebody will."

Gloomy silence fell over them again, until Tom suddenly brightened. "Hey, wait a minute, I've got a flashlight somewhere in the cabin. We can use that to signal for help."

"Great!" Eric followed him down to the cabin, feeling better already. They weren't helpless, after all.

The cabin was so dark they had to feel their way past the furniture to avoid stumbling over it.

"The flashlight's in one of these drawers." Tom rummaged around, found it, and produced a beam of light. "How's this?"

"Let's go!"

They hurried back to the deck, the flashlight's steady beam cheering them, then stood by the rail and shone it out across the water. But even as they did so, they could both see that the light carried only a few feet into the misty night.

"Try S.O.S.," Eric said. "Put your hand over the lens so it makes dots and dashes."

"Okay." Tom flashed it into the darkness. Silence was the only result.

"Here, let me have it." Eric took the flashlight, went to the starboard side, and blinked it there. After signaling several times, they went all around the cruiser, peering into the darkness, blinking their signal until the beam grew faint and they knew no one had seen.

"Got any extra batteries?" Eric asked.

"No. I already looked."

"How about matches, just in case this gives out? We've got to have some kind of light."

"There's matches in the galley."

They went back into the warm stillness of the cabin, and Eric realized how damp and chilly he was. "Wish we'd brought jackets."

"There's got to be a couple in the closet." Tom led the way to the back of the cabin and opened a closet door. "Here." He held out a red quilted nylon jacket to Eric, and put a yellow one on himself. "We can fill up the pockets with matches."

Eric pulled on the jacket. It was only a little too small for him, and it had a warm lining. Then he and Tom went to the cupboard and stuffed their pockets with boxes of matches.

The galley was tiny but well-equipped, with a refrigerator, stove, sink, and even a small microwave oven; everything designed to make the best use of a little space.

"Want something to eat while we're here?" Tom asked. "I'm starving, myself."

"Sounds good. What is there?"

"Take a look in that top cupboard." Tom went to the refrigerator, taking the flashlight with him.

Eric lit a match and held it up to the cupboard. There were several cans on the shelves. He read the labels on two by the flickering light. "Chicken soup!" he shouted as the match burned his fingers and went out.

"There's no way to heat soup," Tom said as he closed the refrigerator door. "They've messed up the whole electrical system. The fridge is off. And I don't like cold soup. Not when we can have . . ." he held the flashlight toward the cupboard as he came to it, ". . . hot chile salsa."

"Yuk!"

"Wait a minute, there's more. Let's see . . . we have green peas, baby oysters, liver paté, and escarole."

"Esca-what?"

"Sounds gross, doesn't it? Let's have cold soup."

Eric grinned. "Cold soup and baby oysters. Got any crackers?"

Tom flashed the beam in the cabinet again and produced a small, square package. "Here you are. And there's some rapidly melting ice cream for dessert."

"It can't be melting too rapidly. It's too cold in here." Eric reached for something to open the soup cans, found an electric can opener on the counter, then remembered the lack of electricity. "Hey," he said, "it's bad enough we're stranded out here without a motor, lights, or navigation equipment, but to leave us without a can opener—that's sadistic!"

"You use a can opener? What's wrong with your front teeth?"

"I'd use my fingernails, but I don't want to spoil my manicure."

Silliness was hitting them, but it felt good, and Eric cheerfully searched the drawers until he found a manual can opener. He took the tops off the two soup cans and handed one to Tom. "Here's to a quick rescue," he said, clinking his can against the one Tom held.

"Yeah," Tom said. "Look out, girls of California, we're coming home soon!" He gulped down some soup. "Come on, we can sit down at the table."

"A table? A real home away from home." Eric fished a spoon for each of them out of the drawer and sat down in one of the chairs at the tiny table. It wasn't until he'd taken some of the soup that he realized he'd been starving, and they finished the food quickly. *If we're still here tomorrow*, he thought, *we might even be happy to eat that stuff that was left. And when it's gone . . . ?*

"You got any fishing gear?"

"Sure, but why do you want to go fishing? The soup isn't that bad."

"Not now. I meant tomorrow."

"Yeah." Tom was suddenly glum. "We might be here for a long time."

"How long can we last, do you think?"

"As long as the fresh water holds out." Tom bit into a cracker. "I don't know how much is left in the tank."

92

"Remember how many boats we saw today? Somebody'll see us."

Tom took the flashlight to the fridge and brought back a quart container of chocolate ice cream. With his soup spoon, he dug into it, then passed the container to Eric. "So what do you think? Did Al send those guys after us today?"

"I guess we won't know that until we get back to La Jolla and find out."

"You still want to try to find out?" Tom sounded pleased.

"Sure. Just because those guys threatened us, I'm not going to back off. We knew it might be dangerous before we started."

"Yeah, but we didn't know just how dangerous. Those two hoods acted like they were in the big leagues. I'm not sure what we're up against. They really might try to kill us next time."

"Well they have to catch us first. And we'll be watching out for them this time. They're not going to take us by surprise again." Eric gave a wistful sigh. "I'm kind of sorry I don't still have the Secret Service guarding me. We'd have Jess and his ugly friend behind bars right now, and you and I would be home."

"You had Secret Service guards?" Tom was impressed. "How come?"

"Because of Gramps. They're with him all the time, and when Alison and I are in Washington, they guard us, too."

"Washington? D.C.?" Tom suddenly made the connection. "*Thorne!* Vice President Thorne is your grandfather? You never told me that before."

"I don't always tell people. Sometimes it's all right, but sometimes it causes a lot of trouble. Like today, for instance. If those men had known—"

"They wouldn't have dared touch us then."

"Or maybe they would have tried to hold us for ransom, or blackmail, or something. You never know."

"Yeah, I guess. But I bet if your grandfather knew where you are right now, he'd have the whole U.S. Navy out after us."

"I wish he did know. I wish somebody knew." Eric got to his feet. "Let's go back on deck. We'd better keep watch for ships."

As soon as they found their way to the stern of the boat and seated themselves, Tom turned off the flashlight. Darkness pressed in around them. It was chilly, with a strong breeze blowing—in spite of the warm days, California nights were always cool. At least the mist had blown away. He looked up at the sky. "Look at those stars!" There seemed to be millions of them, huge and bright. "You know, in the Bible it says, 'The heavens declare the glory of God, and the skies proclaim the work of his hands.' Every time I look at a sky like this I think of how mighty God is. Man! That's fantastic!"

Tom was less impressed. "Yeah. Pretty, huh? See any planes up there?"

Both of them scanned the sky, looking for red and green lights. There was nothing. Eric glanced down at the water, and caught his breath. The ocean was full of lights, too. For a moment he thought the stars were reflecting there, until he noticed that these lights were points of color—red, pink, blue, purple, and yellow—

94

glowing ghostlike under the waves, moving around the ship in a shifting rainbow.

"What's that?" He leaned over the rail.

"I don't know." Tom joined him.

As his eyes became accustomed to the strange display, Eric could distinguish shapes, like luminous torpedos, moving close to the surface, each one a source of many-changing, misty light. He felt as though Earth had turned into another planet. The deep black night, the unusual sky, the dark waves that rocked their drifting boat, and the eerie things in the water gave him an alien feeling.

"Squid!" Tom said suddenly.

"They can't be!" Eric had seen squid before, but none that flashed lights or changed colors. Squid were just plain grey, weren't they? Still, as he studied them, he could see their waving arms and glowing eyes.

"Sure, they're squid." Tom pointed. "Look at that!"

A form sped through the water, heading for the boat, enclosed in an oval, yellow-green halo of radiance. It looked huge.

"That thing must be five or six feet!" Eric gasped. "That's pretty big for a squid, isn't it?"

"Yeah," Tom said uneasily. "I've never seen one that size."

"What do you think they're all doing?" Eric didn't like those waving arms, or the way those weird, lidded eyes seemed to stare at them.

"I don't know. Maybe feeding. Maybe they're just wondering what we are."

"You mean, like, they're thinking?"

"Oh sure," Tom said. "Mom says they have the

nearest thing to a highly developed brain in the whole world of backboneless animals. So does the octopus."

"Yeah?" Eric didn't want to think about that—to believe that those round eyes in the water could be thinking about him. It made this feeling of unreality almost unbearable. He moved away from the rail and looked up at the sky again. Only the stars shone there. But wait—was that a red star, or a red light glimmering high above his head? It was moving! "Tom! Look!"

"What is it? A plane?"

"It must be. Where's the flashlight?"

Tom scrambled for it, then directed the beam upward, blinking it on and off. "He's flying too high. He won't see us." He passed his hand frantically over the lens, making three dots, three dashes, and three dots again, but the faint light barely pierced the darkness. The plane passed. Eric stared sadly at the sky. It was hopeless. Nobody would see them here.

The boat rocked to one side, and something heavy thudded on the deck behind him. Drops of water sprayed the back of his neck. He whirled, and choked with terror as Tom turned.

A huge squid was draped over the side of the boat, glowing luminescent blue-green, its long arms waving close to their feet. Eric drew back to escape them. Tom wasn't fast enough. One of the squid's tentacles whipped around his leg. He screamed and struggled to get free, tearing at the tentacle with his fingers. It only tightened and pulled at him, so that he fell on his back.

Eric grabbed for him, catching him under the armpits, trying to yank him away, but the tentacle held like a vise. He let go his hold of Tom's armpits and pulled at his leg, and when that didn't work, he, too, tried using his fingernails to loosen the snakelike, slimy thing that only gripped tighter. He stomped on it as hard as he could manage, but when he saw arms waving close to his legs, and felt one whip against his back, he backed away, revulsion and fear shuddering through him.

"Help! Help me!" Tom's terrified wail tore through the night.

Eric knew he had to keep out of the way of those squirming arms, but if that other tentacle should fasten around him, then both he and Tom would be lost. If only there was some way to kill that creature! He had to act quickly. The glowing animal was already moving back into the sea, taking Tom with him.

"Help!" Tom shrieked again and struggled, flopping his body over, clawing at the deck.

Eric reached out and grabbed Tom's arms, pulling him back. But it was hard to hold him. The huge squid was trying to drag Tom away! He tugged with all his strength, but the squid was stronger. Tom was inching away, howling in pain and terror, and Eric was losing ground.

He was so absorbed in his struggle, he didn't see the tentacle whipping through the air close to him until it had fastened around his waist and he suddenly felt it tighten. Panicked, he dropped Tom's arms and tried to free himself. As he did so, the squid gave a yank that nearly swept him off his feet. With a supreme effort he held his balance, clawing and tearing at the tentacle that held him.

It was no use. The squid had both of them in a grasp of death.

8 • Suspicions

Through terror-hazed eyes, Eric saw the great squid slowly moving off the deck, back into the water. How could he get himself and Tom free of these tentacles before the beast pulled them into the ocean? His mind, sharpened by fear and the instinct for self-preservation, made split-second calculations. Matches? The flashlight? There had to be something! And as he was thinking, he clawed frantically at the tentacle around him, trying to pry it away. It tightened, and pulled at him. He was being dragged down, losing his balance! He reached wildly for something—anything—to hold onto, but his hands found only empty air. He thudded to the deck, a few feet away from Tom.

Now that the resistance was less, the squid moved faster. The tentacles dragged across the deck, propelled by its undulating arms. Tom moaned, his hands scrabbling at the wood. Eric, his face in a puddle of slime, waved his hands across the clammy surface of the deck in a helpless attempt to find a handhold. But there was nothing . . . nothing to stop their backward slide . . . nothing to help them! He tried not to think of the cold black water, where those shining creatures waited, arms waving, round eyes staring.

Like an echo, something heavy at his feet made a clanging sound. What was it? He could feel it now, his foot pushing against it. With a great effort, he turned his upper body around so that his hands could search for it. There! His fingers found it. Metal. A wooden handle. The hatchet! A flood of relief went through him. He struggled into a sitting position, took a firm hold on the handle, lifted the hatchet, and swiftly brought it down on the fleshy part of the tentacle that lay against the deck beside him. A quiver went through his own body as the squid writhed, but he didn't stop. He chopped fiercely at the tentacle, fighting for his life.

Tom whooped suddenly, "I'm free!" and the tentacle that had released Tom whipped out to stop Eric. He dodged it, then felt it lash at his shoulder and tighten there. He lifted the hatchet and brought it down on the injured tentacle with all his strength, feeling liquid spraying on his face and hands as the blade of the hatchet struck. The coil around his waist loosened suddenly, and he knew he had severed his bond.

The other tentacle pulled painfully at his shoulder. He swung the blade, aiming for the taut portion that stretched out past his shoulder, but as he brought the hatchet down, the tentacle yanked him off balance and the heavy weapon struck a glancing blow off his leg. He howled. The hatchet bounced out of his hands, skidding across the deck.

"Get it!" he shouted to Tom.

"What? Where?" Tom's voice in the darkness sounded bewildered.

"The hatchet. Get it. Quick!"

Eric heard the scrambling sound of Tom looking for it, and he braced himself against the pull of the squid that was moving again, dragging him along with it. "Quick!" he screamed.

He watched the glowing shape, saw the staring eyes, as the animal dropped over the side of the boat, arms writhing along behind it. The tentacle yanked at his shoulder, pulling him over the side! "Stop me!" he shouted as his legs left the deck.

A shape loomed up beside him in the darkness. "Got it!" Tom swung the weapon at the squid's tentacle, and Eric once again felt the quiver that shook even through his own body.

There was the sound of the hatchet dropping, then Tom's hands grabbed his arms, holding him still. "I've got you."

The writhing arms flopped over the side. The tightness in Eric's shoulder relaxed. The tentacle slid away and fell into the water.

Eric lay flat on the deck, breathing hard, feeling as though he could never move again. The pain in his leg was a dull throb. His shoulder ached. The struggle had left him spent.

"Better get up now," Tom said. "There are a lot of squid around the boat. Maybe that one wasn't the biggest."

The idea of meeting another one brought Eric to a sitting position. Tom grasped his hand and pulled him up. Then, using the faint beam of the flashlight to guide them, he helped Eric into the cabin and settled him on one of the couches that served as beds. He kept the light on while he moved around for a few moments, then collapsed on the other couch, across from Eric's, and turned it out.

The boat rocked in the darkness.

"Did you shut up the cabin?" Eric asked, suddenly feeling gooseflesh on his body.

"Yeah. It's closed up tight. But I brought the hatchet in with me, just in case."

There was silence again, while both of them tried to catch their breath and recover from their shock.

"I hit myself with that hatchet," Eric said finally, as a nagging pain in his leg refused to be ignored. He moved his hand to feel the sore place. His jeans were wet—he was wet all over—but just above his knee the wetness felt sticky. "I think I'm bleeding."

"Is it bad?"

"I don't know." He sat up and lit one of the matches from his pocket, holding the flame above his wound. There was blood on his leg, but the fabric of the jeans was whole. He shook the match out. "Guess I didn't cut myself. Just hit my leg pretty hard. That squid bled all over me, though."

"Yeah. All over the deck, too."

"It was close," Eric breathed. "Awfully close." He could still feel the dread he had felt as the squid was pulling him into the water. Goose pimples prickled his skin once more. He was grateful to be alive and have Tom alive and safe with him, and he told God so, praying his thanks.

Waves sloshed against the sides of the boat. There were other sounds, too—vague splashings and thumpings over them and around them. Eric listened, too exhausted to worry, and in a little while he fell into a deep sleep.

The sound of a motor woke him. He opened his eyes and sat up. A faint light illuminated the cabin, and he could see Tom, asleep on the other couch, flashlight and hatchet on the floor beside his bed.

"Hey!" he called. "Wake up! There's a boat out there!" He tried to get up, but a sharp pain in his shoulder and leg stopped him.

Tom opened his eyes. "What?" His voice was slow and sleepy.

"I hear a boat!" Eric tried again to get up, made it to his feet, then found that his leg was stiff as well as sore, and gasped with pain. "Go see what it is," he said.

Tom sat up, looked at him, then got up quickly and went out of the cabin. Eric could hear him shouting: "Over here!" as he slowly and painfully went to join him.

A motor launch was coming full speed toward them, and as it neared, they could see Al Madow at the wheel. Soon he stopped beside them. "You both okay?" he called.

"Sure," Eric called back.

"Yeah?" Al shook his head doubtfully, regarding the wreckage of the *Remora*. In the light of dawn, Eric could see the severed piece of the squid's tentacle, like a gray and twisted rope, lying in a pool of pinkish liquid on the deck. There was a brown substance spattered over everything, and he realized the squid must have squirted ink in the struggle. Tom had blood and ink on his face and hands. Eric knew he must look the same.

Al didn't ask any more questions. He threw them a line so that they could fasten the *Remora's* bow to the stern of his boat. Tom took care of the work involved, while Eric tested his stiff leg and sore shoulder, and found that not only those, but most of his body, ached. When the *Remora* was secured, Tom helped him board the rescue boat. It wasn't until they were seated beside Al in the steering house that he told them what happened. "I've been looking for you since midnight," he said. "And the Coast Guard was looking up and down the coast until I just now notified them I'd found you. When the *Remora* wasn't back in her slip by twelve, I knew something must have gone wrong."

Eric, dazed by pain and these strange events, now wondered why it was Al rescuing them. He and Tom had been sure Al was responsible for those two men hijacking them, but it couldn't have been. Not if he'd been out looking for them all night, worried so much about their safety.

Tom was explaining what happened. He told Al every detail of the story, even mentioning Ben Brightstar, and going on to tell about their brush with death the night before. They were nearly at the marina when he finished.

Al listened, but he asked no questions until he'd heard it all. Then he glanced at Eric. "You hurt bad?"

"I don't think so. Just sore all over."

"We'll get you to the medics right away. Both of you." He brought the boat into the channel, slowing it. "And you have no clue about those two pirates?"

Tom shook his head. "Only a dark red speedboat."

"With the name painted out," Eric said.

"Right. And they wore helmets with visors, and blue jumpsuits."

"And one of them was named Jess."

"That's right," Tom said.

"What kind of speedboat?" Al maneuvered his boat into the slip. "A Scarab? A Cigarette?"

The two boys looked at each other and shrugged. "Don't know," Tom said.

Al seemed disappointed. "I'm going to have to give you a few lessons in watercraft recognition, Son. Thought I taught you better than that." He grinned at them. "And one more bit of advice I'd like to give you. Don't ever let anything you eat try to eat you."

When Al had secured the boat, he brought his car down from the parking lot and picked up Eric and Tom by the gate of the jetty. Then he took them to the emergency hospital. Tom's leg turned out to be mildly lacerated where the tentacle of the squid had held it, but he was otherwise unhurt. The doctor treated Eric's badly bruised leg, after x-raying to be sure no bones were broken. His shoulder and waist, like Tom's leg, bore welts from the suckers that had squeezed them.

"You were lucky you had these sturdy clothes on," the doctor told Eric, holding up the jacket for him to see. Where the tentacle had touched him, the fabric was in tatters.

"I guess I was even luckier I didn't chop up my leg with that hatchet," Eric said. "In that darkness, it was hard to see what I was chopping at."

The doctor tested the bruised leg with light pressure

of his fingers, and Eric winced. "It'll be painful for a while," the doctor told him. "But you'll be fine in a few days."

Eric went home afterward in the MG with Tom.

"Hey, there's my Mom's car," Tom said, pulling into the Kelsey driveway.

Kara must have heard them coming, for she was already at the door, white-faced and worried looking. "Thank God you're both all right!" She smiled at Eric and hugged Tom. "I just got home and phoned Al to see where you were. He told me what happened, and said you were on your way here."

"I thought you'd be gone for a few days," Tom said as they went inside.

"I phoned you several times last night. When it got very late and you still didn't answer, I decided to fly back home on the first plane I could get. My car was parked at the airport, and I phoned Al from there." She sat down on a couch and looked at Eric. "Your uncle is worried about you, too. He asked me to let him know as soon as I found out where you were. Would you like to phone him yourself? Here's the number where you can reach him." She held out a slip of paper.

"I sure would." Eric took the paper. "I hoped he wouldn't find out I was missing, so he wouldn't worry."

"And I'd better call the police while you're doing that," Tom said. "There's another phone in Dad's den. You want to use that line, and I'll use the one out here?"

Eric headed for the den, walking carefully on his stiff leg. He sat down at Steve Kelsey's desk and dialed the number Kara had given him. It turned out to be the number of the hotel where his uncle was staying, and the operator there had to phone several places to try and locate him. "Please stay on the line," she told Eric. "Dr. Thorne is anxious to be contacted the minute you call, no matter where he is."

"I'll wait." Eric glanced idly at the desk. Lying there was the address book they'd found yesterday, the one with the New Jersey addresses, and there was the book that had given them Ben Brightstar's name. He leafed through them as he waited, thinking how dirty and stained his clothes were, and how much he wanted a warm shower. He and Tom had washed their hands and faces at the hospital, but he still felt grubby all over. He absently flipped the pages of the address book. There were sure a lot of numbers in it. Each name had numbers after it, and the phone numbers as well as the street numbers and zip codes were all written neatly and precisely, while the names were merely scrawls. It looked more like a chemistry textbook than an address book, with some of the numbers underlined or in parentheses.

Uncle Walter's anxious voice came on the line. "Eric! Where have you been?"

Eric told him the whole story, making it as brief as he could, assuring his uncle that both he and Too were fine now. "I'll tell you all the gory details when I see you," he said.

Walter Thorne sounded relieved. "But try to stay out of trouble, at least until I get home. All these adventures of yours might make me gray-haired before my time."

"Just think how distinguished you'll look."

"I'd rather wait a few years for that. See you in a couple of days."

Eric hung up the phone and walked slowly back to the living room, wishing his sore body didn't stiffen whenever he sat down. Maybe a hot bath would help that, too. He'd have to get home now and take one, and change into clean clothes that didn't smell like fish.

Kara was coming out of the kitchen. "I'm making some hot soup and sandwiches. You both must be starved."

"Thank you, but I should get home," Eric said. "It's only a couple of blocks. I can walk it."

"Better stay here," Tom said. "The police are on their way. We have to tell them the whole story and all about those two men."

"And I want to hear all about it, too," Kara said. "But first, why don't you both get cleaned up? There are two bathrooms, and Tom, you must have some spare clothes Eric could borrow."

Eric's hot shower felt great. Afterwards, Tom found some pants that fit Eric almost perfectly, and a red plaid shirt, too short in the sleeves, that looked fine when he rolled them up. Eric felt much better when he sat down to eat.

Two policemen arrived just as they finished their meal. They all sat in the living room, the police interrupting frequently while the boys told about the hijacking. One of the men made notes on a pad.

Kara listened quietly, curled up in a big armchair. When the police left, promising to try to locate the two men, but doubtful because of the meager description, Eric and Tom related the adventure with the squid to

Kara. When they had answered all her questions, she spoke to Tom gravely.

"So all this happened because you're investigating Steve's disappearance? Why didn't you tell me what you were doing?"

"Because you've always said he ran off with another woman, Mom, and I just don't believe it. Eric's father said Dad was well-known among conservationists, and that he was working on an important invention. You never told me about that."

Kara's beautiful blue-green eyes widened. "I didn't know anything about it, only that he kept it secret, even from me. I'm surprised anyone else knew about it." She turned to Eric. "Did your father say what the invention was, or exactly what work Steve was doing?"

"He didn't know. He just seemed impressed with Stephen Kelsey and his work. But he mentioned that a lot of his friends thought Steve's disappearance had something to do with his invention."

Kara looked intensely at him for a moment, as though this information shocked her. Then her eyes became guarded and she shook her head. "He's wrong." Now she spoke to Tom. "Eric's father didn't know Steve very well. You didn't know him either. You were just a baby." Her hand restlessly brushed her thick, dark hair away from her pale forehead. "But I knew him very well. He made me believe he was a good man. Hinted at some important work he was doing. But the night he disappeared . . ." she broke off, sighing deeply as though the memory hurt her. "The night he disappeared, he showed his true colors. He was weak and deceitful."

Tom's face distorted with pain. "You don't know that, Mom. You just think he ran off with another woman, but you don't know for sure. Nobody knows what happened to him."

"Believe me, Tom. Believe me, I know." She made a gesture of supplication, palms spread toward him.

Eric, listening to all this, felt embarrassed. It wasn't his business, after all. He stood up. "If you'll excuse me, I'll just go on home now." His voice sounded awkward in his own ears.

"It's all right, Eric." Kara motioned him to sit down again. "I want you to hear this, too, especially since you're involved in this wild-goose chase along with Tom."

The last words stung Eric. After all he and Tom had been through, to call their efforts a "wild-goose chase" seemed outrageous. "Kara, we have good reason to believe that Al Madow might have had something to do with your husband's disappearance."

"Al!" She seemed amused. "Why, Al was Steve's friend and mine. He's been my only friend, ever since. That idea's ridiculous!"

"But he was the only one who knew we were going to see Ben Brightstar yesterday," Tom said.

She turned to him. "And wasn't Al the one who rescued you? The one who notified the Coast Guard when you were out too long? Tom, you're like a son to him. He's never married. You mean as much to him as the child he never had. It's ridiculous to think he'd let any harm come to you, let alone send those two men after you."

"Then who did?" Tom asked, stubbornly.

Kara frowned. "This man, Ben Brightstar, might have. I met him once. He and your father were very close. He might be trying to keep you from finding out where Steve is now." She leaned forward, speaking gently. "Tom, you have to realize that Steve might still be with this woman. Maybe they have other children. They'd have good reason to try to keep you from finding them, or finding out anything about them."

Tom was shocked into silence.

"I'm sorry," Kara said. "But I have to tell you everything now. You're looking for the truth. You have a right to know it, even though it hurts."

Tom, still silent, seemed to shrivel in his chair, but Eric was skeptical. He had four pictures in his mind of Stephen Kelsey, and none of them matched. There was Dad's description of a dedicated, brilliant, well-liked man; Al Madow's words that implied he was a jealous husband and an indifferent friend; the atmosphere Eric himself had felt in Steve Kelsey's den, among his books and family pictures that had made him believe Steve loved his family and friends. Now he was finding it hard to accept Kara's picture. He wanted very much to ask her why she was so sure there was another woman, but he remembered what Aunt Rose had taught him about tact and good manners, and remained silent.

Perhaps Kara guessed his question, or perhaps she had intended to explain anyway, because she settled back in her chair and began to talk. Her voice was low and emotional. Even the passage of so many years had apparently not dulled the pain.

"I married Stephen Kelsey when I was very young," she said. "Young in experience and young in wisdom,

110

at least. I was nineteen, but he was my first boyfriend. My first love.'' She smiled faintly at the memory, but her smile held a tinge of bitterness. ''I thought he was the smartest, handsomest, most wonderful man in the world. And sophisticated. He was eleven years older than I. He'd been all over the world, in the Marine Corps, while I had been sent to boarding schools most of my life. And so, to use the old cliche, I was swept off my feet. He brought me here to La Jolla, to this house. He bought a partnership in the marina. And we were happy—very happy—for nearly two years.''

''Then we decided to have a baby. While I was carrying you, Tom, I found it hard to go surfing and hiking—do the things Steve liked to do—and I had to spend a lot of time resting. I told Steve to go without me. I didn't want to be a millstone around his neck. And so he spent a lot of time away from home. Of course the marina kept him busy, too—and this mysterious invention he wouldn't talk about. By the time you were born, I felt Steve and I were strangers. Of course he denied that he felt that way, too. He told me he loved both of us with all his heart, and called you his pride and joy. I was foolish enough to believe him—to trust him.'' She sighed, then went on. ''You were barely six months old . . . that day.''

''The day he disappeared?'' Tom asked.

''Yes. Our pattern of living hadn't changed much. I was busy with my new baby, and he was busy outside. But that day, he came home for dinner, played with you for a little while, and before he left, he kissed me and told me it was one of the most important days of our lives. He wouldn't explain what he meant. He just told me he'd be back very late and would tell me everything. Then he left us, and he . . . he never came back."

Tom looked confused. "Mom, that doesn't sound like there was any other woman in his life."

The bitter smile came back to her lips. "That's exactly what I thought, honey."

"Then—"

"Wait. I haven't told you the rest. I've never told you this before, Tom, but when Steve didn't get home by midnight, I was very worried. I phoned Al to see if he knew where Steve had gone. He said he didn't, but he came over here right away. I got you out of your crib, and we all went down to the marina to see if the *Kelpie* was there."

"Did Dad tell you he was going out on the *Kelpie?*"

"No, but that was the first thing we thought of. We got to the marina, and his car was parked there. But the *Kelpie* was gone. Al and I waited and waited, but it didn't come in. Finally we called the Coast Guard to search for it." Her eyes misted at the memory, and her voice was a heartbroken sob. No wonder she didn't talk about this often, Eric thought, when it could still make her cry.

Tom sounded sad, too. "But the woman, Mom?"

She brushed the tears away with red-tipped fingers. "I'm getting to that part. It was later—maybe a week later. After we'd given up hope of finding Steve at all. I was nearly hysterical. My mother had to come down from Seattle and stay with us. I was in such a state I couldn't take care of you, Tom, or myself. And Al came to visit us every day, to comfort me, to try to reassure me. But finally he showed it to me. He said if I kept on grieving so much, I'd end up in a hospital. He said I'd better know the truth.''

''What did he show you?'' Tom asked gently.

''What? Oh . . .'' Kara came out of her painful memory. ''I'll go and get it. I've kept it all these years to remind me . . .'' She got up and went down the hall.

Tom glanced at Eric. ''I've never heard this before. Never. I didn't know she felt this way.''

Eric didn't know what to answer, but he knew his opinion of Kara had changed. It was clear, now, she couldn't have played any part in her husband's disappearance. She had spoken too frankly, too emotionally, too convincingly. Unless she was a very good actress. Unless stopping their investigation meant a whole lot to her. But no, she wouldn't put her own son through this kind of pain unless it was honest and necessary.

Or would she?

9 • *White Death*

It was a few minutes before Kara came back to the living room, where Tom and Eric were waiting. She looked more composed now, and had fixed her tear-streaked makeup. In her hand was a yellowed piece of notepaper that she carried carefully.

"Here's how I know there was another woman," she said, sitting down. "This is what Al finally showed me. He found it in Steve's desk at the marina office, a few days after he disappeared." She held up the paper, reciting it rather than reading it, as though she had memorized every word long ago.

My whole life has changed. I'm doing the best thing. It's taken me a long time to figure it all out, but now I'm sure it's right. It's been very hard for me to keep the secret all this time, but I know it will be worth it. Petra is the most important thing in my life.

When she had finished reading and looked at them, the bitterness was back on her face.

Tom looked blank. "Petra?"

"That's the woman's name. Now you know. Your father said it himself. Petra was the most important thing in his life then, and maybe she still is."

"That's a name? I've never heard of anyone called Petra before."

"I have," Eric said. "A girl in my fourth grade class was named Petra. I think her parents were Russian."

Tom stared at him, then shook his head as though trying to clear it. He reached out for the paper. "Can I see it?"

Kara handed it to him. "Be careful. It's brittle now."

"Would it really matter if I tore it?" Tom asked her. "If I threw it away?"

She looked irritated for a moment, then she relaxed. "I guess not. But Tom, sometimes I need to read it again, to remind me."

"To remind you?" He watched her intently. "Why do you want to remember, if it hurts you so much?"

Her eyes flashed in the dimness of the room. "To remind me, in case I ever want to trust a man again."

Eric heard his own breath come out in a gasp, but Tom wasn't surprised. He only looked sorrowful, and read the note. When he was done, he handed it to Eric.

The words on the paper were in a neat, precise handwriting, starting right at the top of the page and continuing to the bottom, filling the whole sheet. "This looks as though it were part of something," Eric said. "As though there should be another page that goes before it, and maybe after it."

"Why?" Kara took the paper from him and looked at it again.

"The way it starts right at the top, with no salutation or date or anything."

"As far as I know, this is the whole note."

"Are you sure it's Dad's handwriting?" Tom asked her.

"Yes. There's no question of that."

"But it isn't addressed to anyone. He didn't even sign it. Maybe it was part of something else, like Eric said."

Kara's eyes blazed again, and she spoke sharply. "I don't know why we have to talk any more about this. It's quite clear to me. It was clear to Al, too. He was very reluctant to give it to me, but he finally decided I should know the truth. If you won't accept it, then I don't know what else I can tell you."

"I'm sorry, Mom," Tom said quietly. "I guess I don't agree with you. I'd like to know a few more things about this note."

"Would you like to ask Al?" Kara said.

Tom nodded.

"All right. We can go to the marina right now. I want to take a look at the damage to the *Remora,* anyway."

They drove to the marina in Kara's Cougar, and found Al in his office. "I thought you'd be coming down to see the boat today," he said to Kara. "I've already phoned the insurance company. They're sending an adjuster around. The Coast Guard and the police want to have a look at it, too, so I've left it be."

"Thanks, Al," Kara said. "Before I look at it, could we talk to you for a minute?"

116

"Why, sure." He pointed out chairs for all of them. "Sit down. You boys look pretty shipshape. How's the leg, Eric?"

"Sore, but I'm getting around on it."

Al smiled at him. "Now what can I do for you?"

It was Kara who answered. "Tom's decided to investigate Steve's disappearance, Al. I guess you know that. So I showed him the note. He wants the truth. I think he should have it."

Al nodded slowly. "I didn't tell you about it myself, Son, since I figured it was your mother's place, if she wanted you to know."

"But I've got some questions about it," Tom said. "Like, where did you find it?"

"Right in Steve's top desk drawer, when I was cleaning out his things to give to your mother."

"I mean, was it part of something else? Were there any more pages like that one?"

"Nope. It was just lying there with the pens and business cards, folded up, like Steve just wrote it and threw it in the drawer." His broad forehead wrinkled. "I kind of figured he might have started to write a letter to your mom before he left, then thought better of it. Maybe he didn't have time, or got cold feet."

Tom leaned forward. "Al, did you know anything about any woman named Petra? Did my dad ever mention her to you?"

Al glanced toward Kara before he answered, as though trying to gauge her feeling before he spoke. "That's the funny part of it, Son," he said. "I did hear Steve on the phone, once, talking about her. I walked into the office, here, when he didn't see me, and heard the name. Didn't mean to eavesdrop, you understand."

"What did he say?" It was Kara who was leaning forward now, surprised.

"It's been sixteen years! I couldn't hold a bunch of words in my brain for that long, not when they mean nothing at all to me." Al leaned back in his chair, scratching his head. "I only remember the 'Petra' part of it because it's a rare sort of name and it caught my attention. And I remember how Steve looked when he saw me there, sort of uneasy, like."

"You mean he looked guilty?" Kara asked.

"That's a good word. Guilty. Like I shouldn't have heard him. But that's as much as I can remember."

Tom leaned back in his chair. Kara sighed.

"Sorry I can't be more help to you, Son," Al said. "And I don't want to let the wind out of your sails, but I think it's pretty plain what happened to your dad."

Tom stood up. "That's okay. Thanks, Al."

They all got up to leave the office, and as they were going outside, Al put an arm around Tom's shoulders. "Let it drop, Son," he said in a voice so low that only Eric, walking next to Tom, could hear. "Let it drop for your mother's sake. She's gone through enough trouble." Then he moved away to catch up with Kara, ahead of them.

Tom caught at Eric's arm, to slow him until the others were out of earshot. "What do you think?" he asked, then. "You're not as wrapped up in this thing as I am. What do you think about the note and everything?"

Eric looked down at the ground, at his toe that was nervously making patterns on the sandy pavement.

118

"You're putting me on the spot. Your mom and Al both told you their story. Don't *you* believe it?"

"I don't know." Tom jammed his hands into the pockets of his cords and gazed across the marina. "I'm just as mixed up as I was to begin with. But I think—I think there was something funny about that note, all right." He began walking slowly again, Eric beside him. "Like, if I was going to leave a note for somebody, I'd start it, 'Dear Whoever' and I'd leave room at the top of the page."

"But it was all there," Eric pointed out, "about how he was doing the best thing, and how hard it was to keep the secret for such a long time, and how much his life was going to change. That was all pretty straightforward."

Tom looked searchingly at him. "Okay. Do you believe it?"

"You want my honest opinion?"

"Yes."

"I just don't know. The note sounds real enough, and it does explain things. But I still don't see why those two guys hijacked us and wrecked our boat."

"Yeah. If Dad's alive somewhere, would he really send somebody to do that to me?"

They had come to the gate of the jetty. Al and Kara were already boarding the *Remora,* moored in a slip near the end of the pier. Eric opened the gate.

"There's another thing," he said. "I think it's very strange the way we keep running into Al every step of the way. I mean, *he* was the one who met that guy so mysteriously, and he was the only one who knew we were going out in the boat yesterday—"

"Except for Ben Brightstar."

"Well, yeah, but we haven't talked to him yet. I think we'd know a lot more if we did."

"That's what I think, too," Tom said. "But I see what you mean about Al. He was the one who rescued us, and he was the one who found the note that was supposed to be meant for Mom. He's right in the middle of it all."

"Sure. But no matter how it looks, he seems to be a real nice guy."

"Right. That's why I feel so mixed up."

"Since you asked for my honest opinion," Eric went on, "I have another thought about that note. I think one reason your Mom didn't question it is because she might have needed to believe your dad was still alive. I think it was easier for her to believe he ran away with another woman than to know he might be dead."

"Man! I never thought of it that way!" Tom looked suddenly determined. "I think we ought to go talk to Ben Brightstar."

"That could be very dangerous."

"Are you afraid to?"

"No way!" Eric paused as they reached the boat, wondering if that were true. The experience on the *Remora* had been pretty scary. But he was so deeply involved in this puzzle now, he knew he would never be satisfied until there was some kind of solution he could accept. And somehow he couldn't accept the solution Kara had offered. There were too many questions without answers.

They climbed on board, joining Kara and Al who were surveying the remains of the steering house. The

120

minute Eric stepped on the deck, all the horror of the night before flooded through him again. At the sight of the squid's severed tentacle, and the pools of blood and ink, he shivered, in spite of the sun's warmth.

Kara looked devastated. "What a mess! I didn't realize . . ." she broke off and turned toward them. "Thank God you're both alive! What you must have gone through!"

"It was pretty awful," Tom agreed. "There's not much left of the boat, either."

"The important thing is that you both got home safely. The *Remora* can be fixed."

Eric gripped the railing, looking out at the boats, trying to compose himself. A sailboat was coming into the channel, reefing its handsome blue sails. And there was a big fishing boat—the one Tom had called "Captain Jack's"—following the sailboat. The three men on it seemed excited, waving their arms and shouting.

Al's voice behind him drowned them out. "Did you give the police the description of those pirates that did this?"

"They came to talk to us," Tom said. "We told them as much as we could."

Eric tried to hear the men who shouted from the fishing boat. It sounded as though they were saying something about a shark. Could it be they'd seen that white shark he'd seen yesterday? He tried to hear, but they were too far away. He watched the sailboat find its berth, and the fishing boat came closer.

Now the shouts caught the attention of the others on the *Remora*. Kara came to stand beside Eric. "What are they saying?"

"Something about a shark."

Al waved at them. "What's up, Jack?"

His voice was loud and must have carried well across the water, because one of the men, wearing a captain's dark blue cap, waved back, "We got a white!"

"A great white shark?" Al was excited.

"Come and take a look!" Captain Jack cried.

Eric felt a hand grasp his wrist, and fingernails pressed into his skin. Startled, he looked at Kara. She had turned very pale, and she was staring at the fishing boat with a look of horror, seeming unaware that she was hurting him.

"He says they got a great white shark," Al said. "Come on. Let's go see."

Al and Tom hurried away, and Eric gently tried to free his wrist from Kara's grasp, but she seemed frozen, her fingers cold against his skin.

"Kara," he said. "Do you want to go see the shark?"

His voice brought her out of her trance. She let go of his wrist and turned quickly, running across the deck.

Eric followed, massaging the place where she'd gripped him. What was the matter with her? He climbed down the ladder and followed the others along the jetty toward the gate.

The fishing boat was heading for the last slip. The shouts of the fishermen aboard were already attracting the attention of others in the marina, so by the time Eric and his friends got there, a crowd of ten or fifteen people had gathered. As they waited for the boat, Eric spoke to Al. "Maybe that shark's the same one I saw."

"It'd have to be. Great white sharks are as rare as horns on a mackerel. I know guys who've been diving off this coast all their lives and never seen one. I've never seen one myself.''

With much excited waving and shouting, the fishing boat pulled into the slip and Captain Jack came to the bow. The crowd moved forward, and Eric saw the flash of a white blouse as Kara pushed her way through. In a moment she was climbing the ladder to the deck.

Captain Jack was talking. ''Now don't everybody try to get up here to look at it. We'll haul it out onto the dock. We have to weigh it, anyway.'

As Kara reached him, he absently stretched out his hand to stop her. Then he looked into her face. ''Oh, it's you, Mrs. Kelsey . . .'' he began, but she brushed impatiently past him.

As soon as Al saw her boarding the fishing boat, he went after her, Eric and Tom following. ''It's okay, Jack,'' he told the captain. ''We'd better go with her, just in case.''

''Well, since it's you, Al, all right. But just the four of you.''

Kara moved quickly toward the stern, her high heeled shoes slipping on the wet deck. She didn't seem to notice.

The shark lay dead, stretched on its back along the starboard side, its once-white belly turning a dirty grey. Eric looked at the open jaws that now hung slackly, and at the bloody head and the blank black eyes. He was sure it was the same fish he'd seen in the marina, even though it looked very different lying here like this. But it was about the same size. The two fishermen who had caught it stood proudly beside it.

Kara looked down at it, her back to Eric.

"That's a white, all right," Al said to the fishermen in his hearty voice. "Where'd you get it?"

"About a mile out," one of the men answered. "We were catching barracuda and yellowtail, and all of a sudden, there he was."

Tom was fascinated. "He just grabbed at your line?"

"That's right. Just swooshed up out of the water and swallowed a yellowtail I'd hooked."

"How do you know it's-a 'he'?" Tom asked.

"See those two claspers by the pelvic fin?" The man pushed at them with his foot. "All male sharks have those. That's how you can tell."

Al eyed the fish skeptically. "It's pretty small for a white shark."

"Eight foot three," the fisherman argued. "I figure it must weigh five hundred pounds."

"More than that," the other said. "You should have seen the fight it put up. Took both of us more than two hours to finally land it."

Kara knelt suddenly beside its head. She stayed there for a few moments, studying it, then got up and walked around to its other side. Now Eric could see her pale, distressed face and her sad eyes. When she finally spoke to the fishermen, her voice was cold. "There's a tag on its dorsal fin. I can't get at it now. When you move it, please remove the tag and send it back to Scripps. The instructions are all inside the dart." She turned and began to walk away.

The two men looked amazed. "How did you know about the tag?" one of them called after her.

She answered without turning. "Because I tagged it."

10 • Where Is Ben Brightstar?

Tom and Eric had no chance to question Kara until they were in her car, driving home. She had left the fishing boat by herself, waited in Al's office for them, then bid Al a hurried good-bye and headed for the parking lot. She was already starting the motor of the car as they got in.

"What is all this, Mom?" Tom asked her. "What's the matter?"

Without answering, she jerked the car into motion.

"Did you really tag that white shark?" Tom persisted.

Her only answer was a nod.

Eric, sitting in the back, caught the faint scent of her perfume. "How did you know it was the same one?" he asked her.

"By its size, and the scar on its snout." The car raced through the gate of the parking lot.

"Hey! Watch out!" Tom shouted as the Cougar veered toward the sidewalk.

Kara braked and stopped beside the curb. "You'd better drive, Tom. I can't seem to concentrate on driving right now."

"Okay." They traded places, and with Tom behind the wheel, the ride went smoothly. "Why are you so upset?" he asked her.

Kara leaned her dark head against the headrest. From the back seat, Eric caught a glimpse of her face, still pale and drawn. When she answered, her voice was tense. "Those two idiots! All they know about fish is how to kill them. They didn't need to . . ." her voice trailed off in a sigh.

"Didn't need to *what? Catch that shark?"* Tom sounded doubtful. "Hey, they're dangerous, aren't they? I mean, think of how many swimmers and divers could have been eaten up by that thing."

"I doubt that. It's been around this part of the coast for nearly a year now that I know of, and it hasn't hurt anyone."

"A year?" Eric was surprised.

"Probably longer," Kara said. "Just because there are sharks in the water doesn't mean people are going to get hurt, you know. Maybe if the shark is big enough, and hungry enough, but not as a general rule. Man isn't really their favorite food."

"Well, I'm not too crazy to meet them," Tom said.

"Of course not. You'd be foolish not to be very careful with them. Especially a great white."

"Yeah," Eric said. "I saw *Jaws.*"

She looked at him over her shoulder. "That was fiction."

"I know, but—"

"There are less than forty documented white shark attacks on record in the whole world," Kara said. "Jacques Cousteau wrote about three instances when he met white sharks and they turned tail and swam away from him. That's fact, not fiction. And I'll tell you another fact. That white shark that we just saw saved my life."

Both boys were stunned at this. "The same one?" Tom asked. "How did that happen?"

"About a year ago, I was out on a Scripps boat with some other researchers," she said. "We were running some tests in the open sea, taking photographs underwater, getting samples, and so on. While we were there, a small white shark got fouled in our lines."

"Small!" Tom interrupted. "That thing looked pretty big to me."

"They can grow to be more than fifteen feet long," Kara said. "By comparison, this one is small. It struggled to get free, but the lines just tightened around its gills. All of us stayed out of its way until we saw it was hanging there, its head down, waiting to die. Well, nobody wanted to cut it loose, of course. But I had an idea. I talked the others into taking the boat to shallow waters so I could wade out and cut it loose."

"Weren't you scared to go near it?" Tom asked her.

"Well, yes. A little. But it was more dead than alive. I tagged it first, then cut through the ropes around its middle. It just lay in the water, dazed, so I gave it a push out to sea. It took several pushes before it finally got the idea and swam away."

"But why did you want to free it?" Tom asked her. "Why didn't you just let it die?"

"Why should we kill it?" Kara asked him. "I don't think we have the right to kill any of God's creatures for no reason. By freeing that fish and tagging it, we had a chance to learn more about white sharks. We know little enough about them now, but they have their place in the scheme of things. They're scavengers of the seas, and they perform useful, vital functions there."

"Anyway, Mom," Tom said, "you saved the shark's life, but how did he save yours?"

"Oh, well it happened the next day. Same ship, same researchers. We were diving near the spot where we'd caught the white, and we saw a bull shark. I was down about fifty feet and didn't like the way it was acting, so I headed back to the ship. Before I could make it, the bull shark came at me. It was coming on fast when all of a sudden, out of nowhere, the white shark appeared. He swam right between the bull and me, heading the other fish off until I could get out of the water."

"Man! That's fantastic!" Tom said. "You sure it was the same white shark?"

"It had the same scar on its snout, and there was the tag I'd put on it the day before. Yes, I'm sure."

Eric shivered at the picture that rose in his mind of Kara and those two sharks. It was almost as unbelievable as when he'd seen her swimming in the kelp bed with those blue sharks. He was beginning to understand her lack of fear that day, but not entirely. She hadn't only been unafraid, but she'd acted as though those blue sharks were as tame as pets. "You mean that white shark would never hurt you?" he asked.

She was silent a moment before she answered. "I can't say that for sure. I don't know. I do believe it was capable of recognizing me, and its debt to me."

"Like Androcles and the lion," Tom said. "Androcles pulled a thorn out of its foot, the lion saved his life in return."

"Something like that," Kara said. "I think any wild creature can understand kindness and respond to it. We might not understand the way they respond, though."

Eric felt confused. So many things had happened in the last few days that he felt he needed some quiet time to himself. He needed to think things out. "Would you drop me off at my uncle's house?" he asked them.

Kara turned to him. "But Walter's going to be away for a while longer. Won't you come and stay with us while he's gone?"

"I appreciate the invitation, but I'd better not. There are a few things I'll have to take care of."

Tom turned down the next street and stopped in front of Walter Thorne's house. "I'll pick you up here tomorrow morning," he said as Eric got out.

And as the Cougar drove away, Eric remembered. Tomorrow they would see Ben Brightstar.

Tom arrived early the next morning. Eric invited him to have some breakfast.

Tom surveyed the scrambled eggs, bacon, and English muffins. "Looks good. I already had cereal and juice, but I guess I could eat some more." He sat down at the table and heaped some eggs on his plate.

"Did you phone Ben Brightstar to tell him we're going out there?" Eric asked.

"No. I don't think we should let him know we're coming this time, do you?"

"I see what you mean," Eric said, biting into his

buttered muffin. "If nobody knows, nobody can try to stop us. But didn't you tell your mom?"

"No. She didn't ask. She just went off to her class this morning. I guess she wouldn't like it if she knew, but she hasn't ever told me to stop investigating." He sipped his milk thoughtfully. "I just figure I've got to find out as much as I can now, otherwise I'll never know for sure about Dad."

"My uncle phoned last night," Eric said. "He didn't say anything about what we're doing either. Just said they found out the yellow stream wasn't toxic and was caused by plankton, so they're coming home. He'll be here later today. I'll leave him a note in case we're not back by the time he gets here."

"We'll go in the MG," Tom said.

"Can you find the place by car?"

"I think so. I've got a route marked on the map."

They demolished the breakfast quickly, cleaned up, and were on their way by nine o'clock, the sun already warm. It was high and hot by the time they reached their destination.

"There's a road along here somewhere," Tom said, "that leads toward the ocean. Can you find it on the map?"

"Sure, it's marked right here."

"Okay, let's watch for it. It isn't a big road."

Finally they found it—a dirt lane just wide enough for one car. They had a bumpy ride through what looked like someone's cow pasture and past a grove of Torrey pines. Finally the road ended not far from a small, rustic house set among trees and bushes, so that it seemed grown there rather than built.

131

Tom stopped the car beside a dusty station wagon standing next to a stone-bordered pond where goldfish gleamed. A large goose flapped angrily at them, then waddled off, squawking. Hens pecked at insects in the dust.

Eric massaged his sore leg. It had suffered during the rough ride, and when he got out of the car it felt stiffer than ever. "No wonder Ben Brightstar told you to come here by boat."

"Yeah. If this is the right place." Tom slammed the car door and looked around.

"Well, there's one way to find out. Where's the front door?"

They walked around the side of the house, following a path worn in the dirt, and climbed the broad wooden steps of the porch. From this vantage point, Eric could see out over the shrubbery. "This has to be the right place," he said, "Look. There's the cove, and the dock and the boat."

Tom nodded and knocked on the front door. They waited, hearing only the gulls' cries and the rustling leaves. He knocked again, harder this time.

There was still no response.

Eric tried shouting. "Is anyone home?"

There was a small clicking sound. The heavy wooden door swung open about three inches, and a girl's voice said, "What is it?"

They could barely see her face in the small opening, but they saw the thick metal chain that fastened the door to its frame so that it couldn't be opened any farther.

Tom spoke. "Is Ben Brightstar at home?"

"No." The girl's voice was cold.

"Are you expecting him soon?" Tom asked.

"Oh, yes. He'll be here any minute now."

"Could we wait for him, then?"

The girl seemed flustered. "No. I mean, he might not be back very soon. He might, though."

Eric laughed. "You don't need to be afraid of us, you know. We're not going to hurt you."

One dark brown eye appeared in the opening and looked suspiciously at them. "Sure. I'll just take your word for that. Why don't you just go away? What do you want with my father, anyway?"

"I talked to him on the phone a couple of days ago. I'm Tom Kelsey."

"Oh." The eyes widened. "I remember. But you were supposed to come here that day."

Tom gave her a wry smile. "We were . . . held up. Couldn't quite make it."

"But we still want to talk to him," Eric added. "Couldn't we just wait for him here?"

The girl seemed uncertain. "I don't know. I guess so. But I'm not supposed to let anyone inside when he's not here."

"That's okay. We can wait on the porch." Eric sat on the porch rail and smiled at her, trying to look harmless and sincere.

Tom sat down on the top step. "Yeah. That's okay."

"But I don't know when he'll be back," the voice wailed. "You can't sit there all day."

"It's very important," Tom said. "We've got to see him. He told me he has some information that I need to know."

Eric got an idea. "If you can tell us where he went, we could go there and talk to him."

The eye in the doorway looked from Eric to Tom. "If you're really Tom Kelsey, tell me what information Father was going to give you."

"It was about my dad, Steve Kelsey. They were friends."

The eye blinked. The door closed firmly.

"We must look like suspicious characters," Eric said.

But the door opened again, this time wide enough to let the girl through. She came out onto the porch. "We can talk better this way," she said, smiling at them.

Eric was pleasantly surprised to see all of her. She was a pretty American Indian girl of about sixteen; her thick, black hair tied in a shining braid. She wore an embroidered blue blouse over her blue jeans, and she was barefoot. "My name's Winona," she said, looking appreciatively at Eric.

"Eric Thorne."

"That's a nice name," she said.

"Thanks. I like yours, too." Eric grinned at her.

Impatiently, Tom broke in. "Uh—Winona . . . your dad?"

She looked reluctantly away from Eric. "Oh—well, the thing is, I'm not sure where he is or how long he'll be gone. In fact, I'm kind of worried about him. He's been gone since yesterday and he's never stayed away this long without calling me." She leaned back against the door, crossing her feet. "See, two men came here yesterday. They told my father they'd found a beached whale. He's involved in conservation. He writes books about birds and whales and things. So they asked him to go with them and see what he could do, since the whale was still alive. So Father went with them in their boat.''

Eric and Tom exchanged startled glances.

"What kind of boat was it?'' Eric asked.

"A big speedboat. Dark red. Why?''

"Oh, no!'' Tom groaned.

Eric felt stunned. This was too much! "Did you see what the men looked like?'' he asked her.

"Not clearly,'' she said. "I wasn't home when they came here. I was just coming back from my girl friend's house as they were all going down to the dock, so I just caught a glimpse of them. When I called to Father to ask where he was going, he came back and told me about the whale. They were getting into their boat.''

"Were they both tall and well built?'' Eric asked.

"Yes. I think so.'' She looked worried. "Why are you asking all these questions?''

"I'll tell you in a minute,'' Eric said impatiently, anxious to be sure before he alarmed her. "Did your dad mention their names?''

"I told you, he didn't know those men.'' Winona leaned her head back against the door and closed her eyes. "Wait. I just remembered. I think he did mention a name. He just told me quickly about it and then went back to the dock, but I can remember what he said.''

"What?'' Eric and Tom waited anxiously, watching her as she frowned, squeezing her eyes shut, trying to repeat her father's words. "He said: 'They saw a live whale up the coast a way, trying to get off some rocks,' and when I asked him who saw the whale, he said: 'Jess and his friend.' ''

11 • Goat Island

Leaning against the front door of her house, Winona looked anxiously from Tom to Eric. "Do you know those men my father went away with?"

"We—we had a run-in with them," Eric muttered.

"They were the reason we couldn't come here before," Tom explained. "They hijacked our boat in the cove out there, then wrecked it and left us stranded out on the ocean."

"Then they lied about the whale?" Alarm distorted Winona's pretty features. "Where did they take my father? What did they want with him?"

"We have no way of knowing," Eric said. "We thought at first that your dad might know them. We even suspected he might have sent them to keep us away from here."

"That's crazy! But they must have come here because of you two. What is this all about? Why do you want to see Father anyway? Tell me!"

Eric tried to calm her. "Tom's father disappeared sixteen years ago. Your father said he knew something about it. We don't know what."

"Yeah." Tom looked up at her from his seat on the porch step. "Do you know what it was?"

"No." She looked close to tears. "I wasn't even born then. How would I know?"

"I thought maybe he'd told you."

Eric stood up. "If Ben's gone with those same two men, Winona, you'd better report it to the police."

She twisted her long braid nervously. "But what do I tell them? I can't describe those men." Then she brightened. "But you can. You saw them."

Tom shook his head. "No. We never got a chance to see their faces. They wore helmets with dark visors so we couldn't tell what they looked like."

"Just tell the police what you told us," Eric said. "And tell them the La Jolla police are investigating the same two men, because we reported them yesterday."

Winona nodded silently and opened the door. Tom and Eric followed her inside. She went straight to the phone, in a little hallway off the living room, and while she made the call, Eric looked around.

The room was bright and smelled of sunshine and flowers. Beautiful, handmade Indian artifacts were everywhere: woven rugs and tapestries, nature paintings and stone carvings, and pottery jars and reed baskets holding colorful floral arrangements. For the first time, Eric wondered where Winona's mother might be, until he saw a photograph in a corner, surrounded by a profusion of flowers. It showed an older Winona—a woman dressed in native costume, serene and lovely.

From the arrangement of blossoms under it, Eric felt sure she must have died.

Tom pointed out to Eric a shelf of books, all written by Ben Brightstar.

Winona came back into the room looking forlorn. "They said I shouldn't worry too much, that Father might just be someplace where there's no phone. They said he'd probably be back soon."

"But didn't you tell them our experience with those same men?" Eric asked her.

She nodded. "They said they'd contact the La Jolla police, but they believe Father's just gone for a little while. They said most missing persons reports turn out that way, and I shouldn't worry until he's been gone at least three days." She sank into a chair. "Anyway, they said they'd talk to the Coast Guard, too. They'll let me know if they find out anything."

"I wish we could give them a description of those men," Eric said. "They'd have something to work with, then. But they probably don't believe the two matters are really connected."

"Well," Tom said, "I'm sure they are."

"So am I." Eric looked at Winona. "Is there anything—anything at all—that might give us an idea of where your dad is?"

She gazed at him despondently. "No. Nothing."

"But you could remember your dad's exact words. You must have a good memory." Eric sat on the couch and tried to encourage her. "Maybe if you close your eyes again and think about how it was—just what happened from the time you got home to the time your dad left—maybe you can come up with something."

She looked doubtful. "You think so? Well, I guess I can try." She settled back in her chair and closed her eyes. "Okay. I walked back from Juanita's house. She just lives about a mile up the road. It was time to make lunch for Father and me. When I got home, I came around the house. I was going up the steps when I heard voices on the path leading to the dock. I couldn't tell what they were saying, but they were strange voices. I turned to look, and there was Father with two men."

"What were the men wearing?" Tom asked.

"One had on a white shirt. I think the other one wore a black T-shirt, and they both had on dark pants."

"Not much help," Tom grumbled. "That's just about what everybody wears."

Eric laughed. "What did you expect? T-shirts with 'We're the bad guys' printed on the back?"

Tom gave him an embarrassed smile and Winona laughed too.

"Sorry about that," Tom said. "Go on, Winona."

"Okay." She closed her eyes again. "So I called out: 'Father, where are you going?' and he turned and saw me. He said something to the men, then ran back here. He said: 'I have to go out for a while. They saw a live whale up the coast a way, trying to get off some rocks.' And then I said: 'Who saw it?' and he said, 'Jess and his friend. They're taking me there to see what we can do for it. I've got to hurry. See you later.' So then I came into the house."

"That's not much to go on," Tom said. "Except that he knew one of their names. Are you sure he didn't know them?"

Winona opened her eyes suddenly. Her voice

sounded faint and impatient. "I know all his friends. They come here all the time. Those men were strangers. Probably they introduced themselves to Father before he went with them."

"But why would he go with them, just like that? Wouldn't he wonder why they were calling on him?" Eric asked.

Again, her tone was impatient. "Everybody knows about Ben Brightstar. People are always calling on him for things like that—injured birds and wounded animals. That's his whole life, and everybody for miles around knows it."

"So we're right back where we started." Tom ran his fingers through his hair. "What now?"

But something was bothering Winona. She looked off into space, a strange expression on her face.

"What is it?" Eric asked her. "Did you think of something else?"

"It's just something silly. Probably nothing."

"Tell us." Eric felt a sudden surge of hope.

"But it's so . . . so dumb."

"Come on!" Tom urged. "Right now we can use any help we can get, even if it's little green men in a flying saucer."

"Well . . . okay. It was just the smell when I came into the house. It was different, and it was very strong at first but it went away after a while, and I forgot about it." She looked at them as though she expected laughter, but both of them were watching her seriously.

"Do you know what the smell was?" Eric asked her.

"Sure. It was the smell of goats."

"Goats!" Tom sank against the back of his chair.

"Do you keep goats here?" Eric was still hopeful.

"No. We used to have one, but it got old and died."

"So the smell came from those men, then?"

Winona nodded. "It must have. I've never smelled goats in the house before. It must have been on their clothing."

"Winona, that smell might just be the clue we need!" Eric grinned at her. "Those two guys must have been afraid we wouldn't pay any attention to that warning they gave us. So they took your dad, to keep him from telling us anything. Probably they're hiding him out somewhere so we can't find him."

She huddled in her chair, looking terrified. "But that means they might kill him!"

"No. I don't think they'll hurt him. They had a chance to kill Tom and me, but they didn't. I don't think they want murder on their hands. They just don't want us to find out anything."

"Wait a minute," Tom said. "How did they know we were going to come here? We didn't tell anybody, or at least I didn't. Did you?"

"No. Of course not."

"Then how could they know?"

Eric tried to think. "Maybe they didn't *know* we were coming here. They just guessed we would. Or maybe—" he broke off, remembering something. "Do you think anyone could have overheard us at the marina yesterday?"

"We were standing beside the *Remora*," Tom said. "That's when we decided. And Mom and—"

"Al!" Eric finished for him, and they both shook their heads.

"Al turns up again," Tom said.

Winona seemed mystified by the conversation. "This isn't helping me find my father," she said impatiently. "What about the goat smell?"

"If they came from someplace where there were goats," Tom said, "then that's where they must have taken your dad."

"At least we can go on that assumption," Eric said, "since it's the only clue we've got."

Winona looked uncertain. "But where would that be?"

"Do you know anyplace they have goats?" Eric asked.

"The McGee's across the cove have some."

"No. They wouldn't hide him anyplace around here. It would have to be a place where there aren't any people to see them, especially since it was daylight when they left."

"And they'd have to be able to reach it by boat," Tom added.

Winona gave a small cry. "There are islands off the coast. Goats live on some of them—wild ones. And they're mostly tiny islands where nobody lives."

Eric was excited. "An island would be perfect! A small, deserted island."

"Are they far from here?" Tom asked.

"They're a few miles out, but we could probably reach one or two of them in about an hour. We could take our sailboat." The excitement that had flared in her eyes suddenly died. "But there are a lot of little islands out there. How do we know which one he's on?"

"We'll just have to search the ones with goats on them," Eric said.

"That could take days!" she said.

"Maybe not. Maybe there are only a few with goats on them. Do you have maps?"

"Yes. On the boat."

"Then we'll start with the closest islands." Eric said. "We've got to try to find him, Winona. At least we can make a start."

"But even if we do find him, what about those men?"

Tom stood up. "We'll figure out a way to handle them. Come on." He reached out a hand to help her up.

Winona, encouraged by their optimism, lingered only long enough to put on a pair of tennis shoes, then led them down to the dock where the sailboat was moored.

They sailed out of the cove, heading into the open sea, Winona at the helm. She was a good sailor, and the ride went smoothly over the peaceful waters, but all of them were tense. They said little to each other, busy with their own thoughts and fears.

Eric was apprehensive. He had tried to sound confident when he told Winona that the kidnappers wouldn't hurt her father, but was that true? What better way to silence Ben than kill him? He prayed that would not be the case, that they would find him alive, and that he would be on one of these islands.

It was mid-afternoon when they sighted a patch of rocky land. All hands helping, they tacked toward it.

Sea birds perched on the rocky heights. Great juts of rock blocked them from moving closer to the island, and so they sailed around it, looking for a place to land. There seemed to be none, until they had nearly circled it, and then they found an inlet where the sandy ground sloped down to the sea. Eric and Tom dropped anchor and they all went ashore in the dinghy.

The island was small—perhaps no more than a mile across. A few scrubby trees, trunks misshapen by the constant winds, huddled near the shore. The three teenagers clambered together over the uneven terrain, searching for any sign of life, but in a few minutes they knew Ben was not there. There was no shelter where anyone could hide. There were not even any goats.

Winona plodded sadly back to the dinghy. "I must have picked the wrong island."

"Let's go look at another one," Eric said. "I'm sure we'll find him if we keep on searching."

"Right," Tom said cheerfully. "He'll be on one of these goat islands. It's the only place that makes sense."

Back on the sailboat, they studied the charts again, found two more islands not far from where they were, and hoisted sail to head for them. In half an hour they were circling another piece of land, not much bigger than the first. This time they could see two goats eyeing them from the crags, but they could see no place where they could land their dinghy safely.

Disappointed, Winona looked at Eric. "How can we search this place if we can't land?"

"We can't. But if we can't land here, chances are nobody else could have, either."

"You're dad can't be here," Tom said.

Just to be sure, they shouted his name, their voices echoing eerily from the dark rocks. Then, in the silence, they listened for an answer. There was only the cry of the birds and the plaintive bleating of goats.

"Let's go on," Eric said. The sun was setting, and they would have to stop their search when it got dark. "The next island isn't far, according to the chart."

By the time they reached it, the sky was already darkening. They were lucky enough to quickly find a sandy inlet where they could leave the boat. Then they went ashore.

As soon as they had walked a few paces across the rocky ground, Winona lifted her head and sniffed. "There it is—that same smell!"

"This might be the place, then." Tom glanced around. "We'd better go carefully."

This island seemed bigger than the other two, and it was shaped like a dome, its slopes covered with sparse green growth. As they climbed the rise they saw several goats that scattered and ran when they came near. Moving as cautiously as they could, they reached the top and looked around.

Eric spotted it first—a boxlike brown shape that seemed to be a building—in a clump of bushes at the bottom of the slope, not far from the ocean. "There!" He pointed, excitedly.

"You think Father might be in there?" Winona was eagerly studying the place, her cheeks red, her eyes bright with hope.

"It's a good possibility, but we can't go rushing down there. He might not be alone, remember."

"I'll bet he's there, all right," Tom said with a confident grin. "This is a perfect hideout! Who'd ever think of looking here?"

"We would!" Winona smiled at him.

"It's almost dark." Eric scanned the terrain in front of them. "We can probably get down there without anyone seeing us. Just be quiet."

His injured leg was hurting him, but Eric ignored it. Winona led the way down the slope, surefootedly navigating the rocky outcroppings. As they neared the building they could see that it was a weatherbeaten wooden shack with a dangerously tilted roof; the one window facing them nearly covered by creeping vines. It looked like a shelter built by fishermen or hunters a long time ago.

They stopped a few feet away from the place and crouched behind the bushes, listening, hearing nothing but their own breathing and the waves washing against the rocks.

"There's nobody here." Winona moaned the words softly.

It was then they heard a man's voice. They couldn't make out his words, but the tone was like a question.

Winona made a small sound of happiness. "It's Father! It really is!" She stood up and started for the shack, but Eric reached out a hand to stop her.

"Wait!" he whispered.

Another man was talking now, and then another. The two kidnappers were in there with him.

12 • Growls in the Darkness

The three teenagers crouched among the bushes beside the crude shack, listening to the voices inside. There were three men, that was clear, and they knew who those men were. Ben Brightstar was with the two men who had hijacked the *Remora*.

Winona was barely able to keep still. "We've got to help Father," she said in a low, urgent voice. "Let's go in there and get him."

Tom glanced at Eric. "We'd better figure out how we're going to do this," he whispered.

"Yeah." Eric shifted nervously. "I wonder if they've got a gun?"

Tom moved closer so he could whisper next to Eric's ear, and Winona, on Eric's other side, could still hear. "They must have a gun. Once Ben found out their whale story was a lie, they'd have to have some way to force him to come here."

Eric nodded in agreement. "But we have the advantage of surprise. They don't know we're here." He knew that was their only advantage. "I've got an idea." He stood up and moved quietly away from the shack, beckoning the others to follow him. In the growing darkness he searched the ground and found a rock small enough to hold in his hand. Without saying a word, the other two got the idea, each of them picking up a stone to use as a weapon. Then they went into a huddle.

"Okay," Eric said in a low voice, "here's my idea." He told them briefly, pointing out where each of them should stand, while Tom and Winona nodded to show they understood. In a moment they were spreading out around the cabin, as silent as shadows.

Eric went past the door, noting the clearing in front of it, then slipped around the corner of the shack. Faint light shone through the cracks in the rotting boards and gleamed in the vine-covered window behind where he stood, but it was dark here. He would not be seen.

This close, he could hear two voices inside clearly enough to distinguish what they were saying. It seemed the two men were playing cards.

"I'll see you and raise you ten," one of them said.

There was a clinking sound.

"I'll call."

"Take a look at these babies."

"Three aces!" There was a muffled curse, then, "Hand me another beer, will you?"

Good, Eric thought. *If they're drinking, they won't be as sharp.* He wondered if Tom and Winona were in position yet. They must be. It was time. He took a deep breath, put his free hand up to his mouth and made a loud, growling sound deep in his throat.

The effect was immediate inside the shack. "What was that?"

"I dunno."

Now another growl came from behind the building, followed by still another.

"Jess! Something's out there!"

"Go take a look."

The door squealed open on rusty hinges. Eric tensed as he saw the man step into his line of vision, then held his breath as a beam of light played over the clearing. The guy had a flashlight. Eric hadn't counted on that, but the plan was in motion now, and there was no stopping it.

He flattened himself against the wall, watching the light move closer. It was close to his feet! *Come on, Tom! Hurry!*

A long, low growl, like the moan of a wounded tiger, tore through the night. The beam of light swung away. Eric hefted the stone he held, then went swiftly, silently around the corner of the shack. The man stood with his back to him, shining his flashlight into the bushes. Eric glanced at the door. It had swung nearly shut. Good! He stole up behind the man, lifted his stone, and brought it down as hard as he could on the back of his head.

The figure lurched forward with a grunt, dropping the flashlight. Eric watched, his heart pounding, as the man staggered and turned to face him. He lifted the rock to hit again, but with a long sigh, like air coming from a balloon, the man crumpled and fell to the ground.

Eric's own sigh of relief was barely audible. He crouched to pick up the flashlight, then froze as the door squeaked behind him.

"What is it, Buck? What's out there?"

Eric's hand drew away from the flashlight. He moved quickly into the bushes as the figure in the doorway, the man who must be Jess, came outside. But as Eric moved, a branch caught his shirt. The rustling made Jess look in the direction of the sound.

"Buck?"

Eric didn't dare breathe. He stood motionless. There was the flashlight on the ground, spilling its beam across the clearing. But it was pointing away from the body of Buck, who lay not far from Eric's feet. Maybe Jess wouldn't see the still form.

"Buck!" Jess called again, still standing in the doorway.

Then Eric heard Tom. The growl he made this time sounded more like a roar. Jess turned toward the sound and hesitated for a moment before he turned back and went inside, closing the door after him.

Eric wondered what to do now. His plan had been to get both men outside, where he and Tom and Winona could surprise them in the darkness. If Jess decided to stay inside, to hold Ben hostage in there, what would they do? He shivered as the night breeze blew cold around him, rustling the leaves. The stone in his hand felt clammy and wet, but it was his only weapon, so he held it tightly, trying to ready himself for anything.

Then someone grabbed at his arm. Startled, he couldn't help the cry that escaped him as he turned. Winona's small figure was standing next to him in the darkness. "I'm sorry. I didn't mean to scare you," she whispered.

"What do you want?" Tension made him gruff.

"What should we do now?"

Eric wondered what to tell her. Maybe they should try to get to that flashlight and switch it off, then pull Buck's unconscious form into the bushes in case Jess did come out again and see it there. He was just about to say so when the door opened again and Jess came outside.

This time he carried a kerosene lamp by its handle, and in his other hand he held a gun. He lifted the lamp so that it illuminated most of the clearing. Eric watched anxiously while he looked warily around, then stepped out a few paces from the door. Now the circle of light shone on Buck's outstretched body. Jess saw it. He gasped, and came quickly toward it.

Winona's small hand grabbed Eric's empty one in a tight, chill grip, as Jess stood looking down at the unconscious Buck, not six feet away from them. He moved the lantern to take a better look, and the light surrounded Eric and Winona. Eric closed his eyes against the dazzle and heard Jess's voice.

"Okay, you two. Come on out of there."

He opened his eyes and saw the gun pointing at them.

They were caught. They had to obey the man with the gun. Eric moved reluctantly out of his shelter, Winona at his side.

Jess eyed them malevolently. "Playing funny tricks, are you?"

"Where's my father?" Winona spat at him. "What have you done with him?"

"He's inside. And you two can come in and join him."

But Eric only stood still, staring at him. Jess was

152

holding the lantern by his side, but there was enough illumination for Eric to make out the thin, pointed face, the dark eyes, and the bushy dark eyebrows. This was the same man he and Tom had seen talking to Al in the park! On a sudden, wild impulse, Eric tried to throw him off guard.

"Aren't you going to invite Al in, too?" he said.

The man's brows made a straight line across his nose. "Al?" he lifted the lantern and turned. "Al's here?"

Eric raised his hand swiftly, hurling his stone toward Jess's head, about five feet away from him. But at the same moment Jess stepped forward, peering into the night. The rock thudded harmlessly on the ground beside him. With the speed of a snake, Jess turned back, glaring at Eric. Cursing, he leveled the gun at him, and for a terrifying moment, Eric knew he was going to fire it. Instead, it flew out of his hand, the lantern dropped, and Jess's face crumpled into an expression of pain before he sank to his knees with a howl.

"Get his gun!" Tom shouted, and for the first time Eric saw his dark figure just behind Jess.

He dived at the gun, grasping it where it lay in front of the stunned Jess. Then he backed quickly away, pointing the gun with a shaky hand.

Winona came up beside him. She looked at Tom and then at the injured Jess. Then, with a loud sob, she darted past them, running toward the shack.

Eric felt as though he might sob, too, but instead he heard himself whooping with relief and surprise. "Talk about the nick of time! Man, am I glad to see you!"

Keeping his eyes warily on Jess, Tom moved into the light of the still-burning lantern, breathing hard. "Hit him as hard as I could," he panted. "He should be knocked out."

Jess moaned loudly.

"You did just fine," Eric said.

"What was that you said about Al? Just as I was creeping up behind this guy, I heard you say something about Al and then he turned and nearly saw me. I had to dodge fast to keep from getting caught."

Eric was too shaken to explain. "Take a look at him," was all he could say.

Tom looked down at Jess, who had collapsed into a sprawl, his hands holding the back of his head, his eyes squeezed shut in an expression of agony. "It's the same guy!" Tom gasped.

"Yeah. That guy we saw with Al." Eric was still shaking, but now he was able to think. "What will we do with them?" He nudged the leg of the unconscious Buck with his toe. "This one might come to any minute now, and Jess here could decide to ignore his headache and put up a fight."

"If you'll keep the gun on them, I'll see if I can find something to tie them with." Tom hurried across the clearing toward the shack, but in a moment he was back. "It's pitch black inside there. Winona seems to have found her dad all right. I can hear them talking. But I'll need some light."

"Better not take the lantern," Eric said. "I need that right here. But there's a flashlight over there, if it still works."

Tom found it and picked it up. The beam was still shining steadily. He took it back into the shack.

Now Eric could hear Winona's questions and the answering voice of her father. Both of them sounded happy. When Tom came out of the shack, they were right behind him.

"One thing they've got lots of in there is rope." Tom held up a coil of what looked like braided nylon.

Ben Brightstar, a stocky, dark-haired man in a plaid shirt, came into the light. "All that, plus the rope Winona just untied from my hands and feet." He looked down at the writhing figure of Jess. "Let me help tie them," he said. "It'll be a pleasure."

While Eric held the gun, Tom and Ben tied Jess's feet and hands securely. Then they went to work on Buck, accompanied by threats and mutterings from Jess, who seemed to have forgotten his head wound. When they were through with their task, Winona picked up the lantern.

"Let's go inside," she said. "I don't like the company out here."

The shack had four rooms, which Eric found surprising for such a small place. Besides a tiny kitchen and bathroom, there was a bedroom behind the front room, and it was there Ben had been kept. "They had me trussed up like a mail-order package," he told them, his broad, gentle face beaming. "And they were going to leave me here like that tonight. They were just waiting till it got dark before they went back to the mainland. Said they'd come back once in a while to feed me, but I'd hate to have to count on their promises!" He shook both Eric and Tom by the hand, clapping them heartily on the back as he thanked them. "I don't know who you are or how you found me, but I'm mighty grateful you did. Mighty grateful!"

"It was the goat smell," Winona said, looking at her father with shining eyes. "And these are my friends, Eric Thorne and Tom Kelsey."

"Kelsey? Of course! I should have known you. You look just like Steve."

"We went to your house to talk to you about Dad," Tom told him. "That's when Winona told us you'd gone away with two men. We finally figured out they must be the same ones who hijacked our boat a few days ago when we were coming to see you."

"You know them?" Ben asked.

"No, but they seem to know us."

Eric spoke up. "We think that's why they brought you here, to keep you from telling us what you know about Steve Kelsey."

Ben looked bewildered. "Was that it? They wouldn't tell me anything—not one thing. Just said they were keeping me here until they decided what to do with me. But Steve . . . why, he's been gone fifteen or sixteen years now. Why would they—" he broke off and put an arm affectionately around Winona. "Tell you what," he said. "We have a lot to talk over, but not here. I've had enough of this place. Let's go home."

Eric and Winona agreed with that idea, and even though Tom looked disappointed, he went along as they left the shack. "Should we try to take these two along with us?" he asked the group as they went outside.

"It'll be safer if we leave them where they are," Ben said. "We'll call the Coast Guard on the ship's radio. Let the authorities take care of them."

"Okay," Eric said. "Then let's go see what we can get out of them before we go."

Buck had regained consciousness, but he still lay flat on his back. His eyes glittered in the light of the lantern, as he looked at them. Jess was sitting up, straining to get free.

Eric knelt beside him, trying to decide how to question them. Maybe if he gave them a chance to blame someone else, they might talk. "Who got you two into this mess?" he asked Jess.

The man only glared silently at him.

Ben tried. "I don't know you, and you don't know me," he said reasonably. "Who sent you to kidnap me and hold me here?"

"Untie us and we'll tell you," Jess said.

"Sure," Buck added. "Let us go and we'll talk."

"No," Ben said. "If you don't talk to us now, you'll have to deal with the police."

Tom stood in front of Jess. "Eric and I saw you talking to Al at Mission Bay. We know he must be mixed up with you some way. Did he send you out to get us?"

"Al? Jess looked surprised. "Who's Al?"

Eric stood up. They weren't going to learn anything from these two, and he was bone tired and very hungry. "Let's go," he said. "They'll talk to the police."

Winona, holding the lantern, led the way. "I keep thinking about that platter of enchiladas I made this morning. They're still in the fridge, along with a chocolate cake and a gallon of milk . . ."

Buck groaned.

"Don't worry," Ben called to him. "We'll treat you better than you were going to treat us. The Coast Guard will come and get you. They might even feed you."

Eric headed up the slope beside Winona, Tom and

Ben following them. The two men shouted curses and threats after them, but they trudged on without pausing. In a few minutes the voices were only distant murmurs.

They found the place where they'd left the dinghy, and rode over the low swells to the sailboat. As soon as he was on board, Ben went to the radio to call the Coast Guard. While the others secured the dinghy to the stern and hauled up the anchor, he told his story and gave the location. Then he switched off the radio and turned to them. "We're going to have to wait until they get here. They say it'll be a few minutes. They've got a patrol boat not far from here."

"Well as long as we're waiting," Tom said, "could you tell me about my father? I know you've been through a lot tonight. I guess we all have. But it's really important to me."

"It's a mighty long story, and it's not a pleasant one," Ben said. "Let's wait till we get home and get fortified with some of Winona's food. Then I'll tell you whatever you want to know."

13 • The Invention to Change the World

The clock in the kitchen of the Brightstar home showed half past ten.

Eric breathed in the scent of the enchiladas Winona had put in the oven to heat. They smelled like chili and melting cheese, and he was starving.

Winona smiled when she saw his expression. "It'll be ready in a couple of minutes. I wonder if those kidnappers have told the police anything yet?"

"They sure wouldn't talk to the Coast Guard." Eric thought of how silent they'd been on the island after the Coast Guard had taken statements from him and his friends. They'd even boarded the patrol boat without protest. "I don't know," he said to Winona. "Maybe we'll never find out who they are or why they did all this."

"Want some milk while you're waiting?"

"Sure. Thanks."

She poured a large glassful and was handing it to him

159

when Ben and Tom came into the kitchen.

"Well, that's done," Ben said. "We told the police everything, and the Coast Guard turned in their report when they handed those guys over. All we have to do now is to go to the police station in the morning and make out complaints against them."

Winona poured milk for all of them. "I was hoping I'd never have to look at those two again."

"It can't be helped." Ben went to a cupboard and took out some plates. "Here, let's set the table so we can dig in." He handed china and silverware to Eric and Tom. "By the way, you two should plan on staying here tonight. It's late now and we could all go to the police station together in the morning."

They set the table in the wood-paneled dining room, then Tom and Eric went to the phone in the little hall-way.

Tom seemed reluctant to make the call. "Mom's not going to like this. Here we are still investigating, and still getting into trouble."

"I know," Eric said. "I'm hoping there's no hassle when I talk to Uncle Walter. You want to go first?"

"After you."

Uncle Walter was home, and anxious about him. Eric explained, as briefly as he could, what had happened and what they had to do in the morning.

Surprisingly, his uncle sounded pleased. "As risky as it was, you did the right thing. Catching those crooks took brains and courage. You can tell me all about it when I see you tomorrow."

Eric hung up feeling much better, but Tom didn't fare as well. Kara must have been upset, because when he was through with the call, Tom was frowning. "But I think she understands," he told Eric. "She didn't ask me to stop. Just told me to keep in touch."

Winona appeared in the doorway. "Dinner's on the table."

At first they were all too busy eating to talk, but while they had second helpings the three teenagers explained to Ben how they'd found him, and he related his adventures with the kidnappers.

Finally Tom, who'd been waiting impatiently for the chance, brought up the subject of his father. "Tell me now, Ben. Tell me about Dad."

"He was a good man. A good friend. I never knew him to be mean or cruel. He treated everything and everyone with respect and love."

"That doesn't sound like he was weak or deceitful." Tom jabbed his fork into his enchilada.

Ben munched on a tortilla while he thought this over. "Weak? Not unless consideration and care are weaknesses. He did keep his own business to himself, but I wouldn't call that deceitful."

Eric had a question of his own. "Did you know about an invention he was working on?"

"Oh sure. There were several, but I know the one you mean. Steve was a brilliant inventor, and his last discovery was something that could change the world."

Eric, Tom, and Winona asked the same question at once. "What was it?"

Ben took another bite and chewed it before he answered. "I don't know the whole story of it, but I can give you the broad idea. He was testing kelp, extracting some chemicals from it, working out formulas. One day he showed up here, mighty excited. He said he knew he could trust me and he had to tell someone. He said he'd found the formula at last. He discovered a new fuel, made from kelp, that would replace gasoline."

Exclamations went around the table.

"You mean like a new energy source?" Winona asked him.

"That's right. A cheap, clean new fuel that wouldn't cause pollution. It couldn't harm the environment at all."

"And it could replace gasoline?" Eric was amazed.

"Steve said he'd tested it, and all the tests worked out just fine."

"But why did he want to keep it secret?" Tom asked. "Why wouldn't he want to tell everybody about it?"

"He said someone was spying on him. There are some folks who'll do anything to keep that kind of thing off the market, you know."

Eric nearly dropped his fork. "Spying on him? Did he know who it was?"

"No. At least if he knew, he didn't tell me. Just said he thought his life was in danger, that somebody wanted to stop him."

"So that's why he didn't even tell Mom!" Tom murmured. "She didn't know anything about it."

"Steve wanted to keep his family safe," Ben said. "If your mother knew about the formula, she'd be in the same danger."

"But she said he was lying to her—keeping secrets from her, and all the time there was a good reason." He reddened slightly as he looked at Ben. "She thought there was . . . some other woman."

"I don't think there was. Steve never mentioned anyone to me, but he talked a good deal about his wife and his baby son, about how wonderful they were."

Tom's face grew even redder, and his voice was wistful. "I wish I'd known him."

In the silence that followed, Eric's thoughts whirled. "Ben, do you think this invention had something to do with Steve's disappearance?"

"Of course." Ben glanced at Tom. "Sorry, my friend, but I warned you this wasn't a pleasant story."

"I want to hear it. I've got to know whatever you can tell me."

Ben smiled. "Good. You're a lot like your father, Tom." He settled back in his chair. "I saw Steve the morning of the day he disappeared. He came here to ask me a favor. He wanted me to go with him that night. Said he had talked to a government official—that they'd arranged a secret meeting to show him the new fuel. He wanted to give it to the U.S. government so it could be developed properly and used the right way."

He looked sad, now, as he remembered. "So he asked me if I'd go with him to that meeting. He felt someone might find out about it and try to use force to stop him. Two of us could handle that better than a man alone. I've always been sorry that I couldn't go with him. I couldn't leave my wife that day. I had to take her to the hospital. You see," he looked fondly at his daughter, across the table, "Winona was born that night."

Winona looked sad, too. "My mother lived only three days after that," she added.

Ben nodded, grief on his face. "It was a sad time, but

Winona was there to ease the loss of my wife and my best friend." He looked up at Tom. "But I wish I'd been free to go with Steve that night on the *Kelpie*. Whoever was spying on him must have found out about that secret meeting. They went after him. I believe they must have killed him and stolen the fuel samples and the formula, because in all these years I've never heard anything more about it."

"But if somebody stole the fuel samples and the formula," Eric said, "wouldn't they try to make money on it?"

"Not if they had an interest in keeping the new fuel off the market, like I said."

"But who would want to keep it off the market?" Tom asked.

Eric suddenly knew. "Oil companies, of course. They wouldn't want anyone to discover something that could replace gasoline. They'd have to go out of business."

"That's what I suspect," Ben said. "But I don't have any proof. And after all these years, I don't think there's any."

"But what about those two guys who kidnapped you?" Tom said. "They tried to keep you from telling us about this. They must be the ones who were after my dad."

"Or they know who was," Eric said.

"Yeah. When the police make them talk, then we'll know." Tom looked excited.

"Not so fast," Ben said. "We're just guessing at this, remember. *If* those men are the guilty ones, and *if* they were hired to kill Steve, chances are it would have been some oil interests, with lots of money behind them. So they'd also have plenty of money to bail them out of jail and hire smart lawyers to get them off. Those two guys won't be worried, and they won't be likely to tell us or the police anything that would involve them."

"They sure didn't seem worried," Winona said.

"We can tell the police what we suspect," Ben went on, "and hope they'll investigate. But since Steve disappeared such a long time ago, I don't think they'll be interested."

Tom was looking thoughtful. "Why didn't you ever tell my mother all this, Ben?"

"I tried to. I phoned her a couple of weeks after Steve disappeared, after I realized something bad must have happened to him. I suppose I should have called her right away, but there was so much happening . . ." He shrugged, then went on. "Even then I wasn't sure I should tell her about the invention, since Steve had told me she'd be in danger if she knew anything. So I just told her I'd like to talk to her about Steve. I was going to tell her I knew where he was going that night, so she could tell the police where to look for him." He shook his head. "But I never got to tell her anything. She said she didn't want to see me, or any of Steve's friends. She sounded mighty upset. Then she told me she had a note from Steve, telling her where he was going. She wouldn't discuss it any further." He looked at Tom. "There wasn't anything more I could say. I didn't even go to the police after that. I thought your mother knew more than I did about the matter."

"Yeah," Tom said. "She showed us that note. It was kind of strange, but she believes it."

"What did it say?" Winona asked him.

"Something about how some woman was the most important thing in his life."

"Well then," Ben said, "it seems we're wrong, doesn't it? All our guessing must be wrong."

"Ben," Eric said suddenly, "did you say you could tell the police *where to look* for Steve?"

"Well, I know where he was going to meet that government official, but—"

Eric and Tom looked at each other, wide-eyed.

"Where?" Tom nearly shouted it.

"Well, as a matter of fact, it was Goat Island, where you found me today. The place is a perfect spot for a secret meeting. Nobody ever goes there anymore."

"But Jess and Buck knew about it," Eric said.

"I wondered about that, too," Ben said. "It's mighty strange they'd take me there. Almost too strange to be a coincidence. But if Steve left a note . . ."

"I think that note was a phony," Tom said. "Both Eric and I thought so when we saw it." He leaned on the table, looking eagerly at Ben. "Let's go there again and see if we can find any trace of Dad."

Ben looked doubtful. "If our idea is right, then I don't think he ever got to the island. I'm pretty sure the government man he was going to see wouldn't be waiting there for him alone. He'd have special agents with him, to protect himself and Steve as well as the invention. If Steve got to the island that night, they'd know about it."

"Yeah," Eric agreed. "And when he didn't show up for the meeting, they'd start their own investigation to find out why. So they couldn't have discovered anything or they would have told the police and Kara.''

''But we know Dad took the *Kelpie* out of the marina that night. Whatever happened to him, happened between there and Goat Island.'' Tom wrinkled his forehead. ''Maybe they hijacked the *Kelpie*, took the fuel samples and sank the boat out in the ocean. We'd never be able to find it!''

Eric thought for a minute. ''They wouldn't sink the boat in the regular ship channels. There'd be too much danger of somebody seeing them.''

''That still leaves a lot of ocean.'' Tom looked dejected.

They all were silent. It seemed they'd come to a dead end, Eric thought. In spite of this new information, they had no proof, and no way of getting any.

Winona passed around slices of chocolate cake. ''Here. This won't help you think, but it tastes good.''

Tom took a listless bite, then spoke: ''Unless we can think of something, I'll never know for sure about Dad, and Mom will always think he ran away with another woman.''

''And that new fuel will be lost forever, too,'' Winona added.

''I've got to try to find his boat somehow. There's got to be some evidence on it.''

Ben was frowning. ''I've just remembered something mighty strange. Something Jess and his friend said when they took me to the island.''

Everyone looked at him.

''When they brought the speedboat in toward the land, Jess was holding the gun on me and Buck dropped anchor out by some rocks. Jess told him to be careful.

167

He said something like: 'We don't want it to hook onto what's down there and bring it up,' and then both of them laughed as though that was mighty funny.'' He looked from Tom to Eric. "I didn't even think about it at the time, but now I wonder—do you think he could have meant Steve's boat?"

"Maybe that's it!" Tom said eagerly.

But Eric had doubts. "If they sank the boat that close to the island, what about the people waiting there that night? Wouldn't they have seen it?"

"I don't think so," Ben said. "It was beside a sort of rocky point of land. The rocks were high enough to hide any lights or sounds from anybody on the island who might be watching."

Eric looked at Tom. "If we take our scuba diving gear out there—"

"We can dive down and see!" Tom was enthusiastic.

"Okay," Eric said. "It's worth a try, anyhow."

Ben raised his voice to be heard over their excited talk. "You can't do that. The waters around the island are full of sharks. Big ones." He stood up and glanced at his watch. "It's after midnight. We'd better turn in. You boys come along and I'll show you to your room."

He led them to a spare bedroom at the back of the house, and bid them goodnight. Eric sank onto one of the twin beds. His sore leg had been ignored in this excitement, but now it felt stiff again. "I'm so tired, I don't even want to get undressed," he said.

"Me too." Tom dropped on the other bed and stared up at the ceiling. "But I don't care what anybody says. Sharks or not, I'm diving. If the *Kelpie's* down there, I'm going to find it."

14 • The Sunken Ship

It was late the next morning, after their visit to the police station with Ben and Winona, that Tom and Eric got into the MG and drove back toward La Jolla.

The visit to the police hadn't been cheerful. They'd had to give statements, identify the two men, sign complaints.

"And the police think the same thing Ben does," Tom said. "They told me Jess and Buck are already in touch with their lawyer. He's going to bail them out as soon as he can. They aren't going to talk until they go to trial. *If* they get to trial. Even though it's a federal offense to kidnap somebody, and even with all of us as witnesses, they might get off anyway."

Eric knew this was true. "It's hard to believe," he said. "If only we had some evidence—proof they were the ones who hijacked the *Remora*, and proof that they were mixed up with your dad's disappearance."

"There's not much use trying to get anything out of Al," Tom pointed out. "He'll just deny that he knows them. It's his word against ours."

"And the police say evidence is the only thing that can help," Eric said. "So I guess we have to go diving for your dad's boat."

"And hope the sharks aren't hungry."

Eric absently rubbed his bruised leg. It hadn't been stiff when he got up that morning, and all the time they'd been at the police station it had only twinged once or twice. It was healing. At least that was good news. "What was Winona telling you about having a party?"

"Next Saturday, I think. Anyway, she said she'd call and remind us the day before." Tom turned the car onto La Jolla Boulevard. "Maybe we'll have all the evidence by the time we see her and Ben again."

Eric wasn't too sure, but he tried to sound confident. "At least we'll find out if the *Kelpie* is there. You still want me to go home with you?"

"Sure do. I need you to help me explain Ben's story to Mom. If two of us tell her, she might even believe it."

"Okay, but let's stop at my uncle's first so I can change clothes and say hello to him."

They found Walter Thorne on the terrace, reading. He looked up when he heard them. "Well, you two look healthy enough after all the adventures you've been through. Sit down and brief me on the latest." He waved them to seats.

"Is it okay if Tom tells you everything while I change?" Eric said. "Being an adventurer is hard on

170

clothes, I've found out. My designer jeans are getting torn up.''

''Those are designer jeans?'' Walter stroked his beard. ''I thought frayed denims must be coming back into fashion. Sure. Go ahead and change.''

From his bedroom, Eric could hear the murmur of voices on the terrace as Tom talked with his uncle. When he joined them a few minutes later, Tom was telling about the *Kelpie*.

''So Eric and I have decided to dive at the place Ben described near the island. We're going to find out if the *Kelpie's* really down there, and get whatever evidence we can.'' Tom wasn't going to mention the sharks.

Walter thought this over. ''I suppose there's no use trying to talk you out of it?'' he said finally. ''I know how much this means to you, Tom, but your search might be a waste of time. Or, on the other hand, you might uncover something you don't like.''

''I know that.'' Tom looked out across the sunlit sea. ''But if I don't, I'll have to live with this question for the rest of my life. And those two goons will probably get off and go out and kill again.''

''Besides,'' Eric said, ''there's the invention. Did Tom tell you about it? The new fuel?''

His uncle nodded. ''If that's true, whoever stole it ought to be locked away for good. The whole world needs it.'' He looked at Eric. ''When are you planning to make this dive?''

''As soon as we can.''

''All right. I'd like to go with you. And since your boat isn't in any shape to travel, Tom, we can use mine.''

171

"That would be great."

"Fine. Then let's go out tomorrow morning early. An operation like this one needs lots of time and daylight."

Later, as they were heading for Tom's house in the MG, Eric had second thoughts. "Maybe we should have told my uncle about the sharks around the island."

"I don't think so. This way he won't find out until we're there, and it'll be too late to change the plan. Besides, I'm not afraid, are you?" He didn't wait for Eric's answer. "Ben could be wrong, anyway. Maybe there aren't any sharks out there at all."

They parked the MG behind Kara's car in the driveway and went into the house. She was in the kitchen. "I'm baking cookies and a cake," she said, smiling. "Thought if I made enough good things to eat, you'd stay home and eat them."

Tom grinned at her. "I'm not going anywhere, Mom. At least not today."

"But tomorrow? The next day?" She stood back, surveying them, an apron over her red dress, a wooden spoon in her hand.

"Tomorrow morning we're going to dive to try to find the *Kelpie*."

"*What?*"

So once again Tom and Eric had to tell the whole story, sitting around the table in the breakfast nook, munching on cookies as they talked. When they were through, Kara looked bleakly at them.

"I don't believe it. I know what happened to Steve. Ben Brightstar is wrong. Did you ask him if he knew anything about this Petra woman?"

"Yes. He said he didn't ever hear about any other

woman," Tom said. "And Mom, what about the men who kidnapped him? They were the same ones who wrecked the *Remora*. How do you explain that? Why would they do all this if Dad just went away with someone else?"

She looked at him for a long, uncomfortable moment before she spoke again. "Well, this idea of yours that Al is mixed up with them is ridiculous, I'm sure of that. But all right. There's just one way to find out the truth. If you two want to look for the *Kelpie*, I want to go with you. But Tom, if we can't find it, I want you to give up this investigation."

Tom didn't hesitate. "I promise," he said.

It was just after dawn the next morning when they all met at the marina with diving gear and equipment. Tom was bursting with excitement, but Kara seemed cool and greeted Eric and his uncle with a frosty smile.

"This is a wild goose chase, Walter," she said. "But the boys won't listen to me."

"Well, whatever happens, it's a beautiful day for a swim." Walter smiled down at her and fell into step beside her as they walked through the parking lot toward the dock.

Watching them as he and Tom walked behind them, Eric had the feeling that his uncle was happy just to be spending the day with Kara Kelsey. He could almost understand that. She was certainly beautiful, dressed today in a crimson jumpsuit, her masses of long, dark hair curling over her shoulders. Too bad she didn't like his tall, handsome uncle. They were a good-looking couple.

As they walked between the two buildings, a shout interrupted his thoughts. Eric saw Al hurrying toward them.

Tom reached out to touch his mother's arm. "Don't tell him where we're going, Mom. Please."

Kara looked over her shoulder at him. "Oh, all right," she said reluctantly.

"Good morning," Al called as he neared them. "You're here bright and early today! How are you, Kara . . . Dr. Thorne?" Eric noticed the hint of surprise on his face as he recognized Uncle Walter. "And there's my two favorite helpers!" Al's voice was hearty, as usual, but Eric was sure he detected something different in his expression and manner. When he felt Tom's elbow nudge his ribs, he knew Tom had noticed it, too. But of course, if their ideas were right, Al would know about Jess and Buck's arrest by now. And he'd know who had caught them.

Tom's voice was silky. "Hi, Al. We're not here to help today. Going out to dive off La Jolla coves."

"Oh?" Al raised his eyebrows, watching their faces intently. "Well now, that's a shame. I was just going out to catch some yellowtail. You'd all be welcome aboard."

Kara smiled at him. "That's nice of you, Al, but we've already made other plans."

"Yeah," Tom added. "Thanks anyway."

Walter and Kara were already walking toward the jetty, and Al joined Tom and Eric.

"How's the leg, Eric?"

"A lot better, thanks. The swelling's gone down so I don't even feel it any more."

174

Al draped a hand casually over Tom's shoulder. "And how about you, Son? You all recovered from your fight with that squid?"

"Oh sure, Al. I'm fine."

Al was walking more slowly now, Eric noticed, and he and Tom were forced to slow, too. Walter and Kara were already going through the gate, a few yards ahead.

Al's voice dropped to a murmur. "Listen, boys, I've been meaning to tell you something. Wait up a bit, here." He stopped, and Tom and Eric turned to face him. "You know that friend of Steve's you were aiming to see? The Indian . . . Ben Brightstar?"

"Yes?" Tom looked at him warily.

"Well now, I got to remembering something. It slipped my mind when you mentioned him before, but I recall it all now. I figure you should know about it. You see, he's crazy."

"Crazy?" Eric echoed.

"What do you mean?" Tom asked.

Al scratched his balding head. "Well, you see, there was this big deal about him a few years back. Seems he went berserk and nearly killed some other Indian in a bar. You know how Indians get when there's firewater around." He smiled and winked. "Anyway, they hauled this Brightstar into the slammer. Well, it turns out he's not dealing with a full deck, so they had to put him in the loony bin for a while. Guess he's out now, running loose on the streets."

Tom and Eric stared at him, wordlessly.

"So I figured you ought to know," Al went on, "so you won't waste your time on him."

Tom gulped. "Uh . . . thanks."

"Sure. Don't mention it." Al waved cheerfully and walked away.

When he was out of earshot, Tom moaned. "Do you think that's true?"

"I sure hope not." Eric walked slowly toward the gate. "I sure do hope not. He didn't *seem* crazy."

"No. He seemed like a real nice guy, but then, you can't always tell, can you? I mean, how would you know?"

Eric could only shake his head. He didn't know. But there was no time for more speculation. Kara and his uncle were already climbing to the flying bridge of the sleek white motor yacht, getting ready to take them out to Goat Island. All Eric and Tom could do now was climb aboard.

"Al could be lying," he said to Tom when the boat was moving into the channel. Kara sat beside Walter at the controls and the two boys in passenger chairs a few feet away.

"Yeah, he could. But that's a big lie, saying some-body's crazy. He sounded like he knew all about it."

Their confidence shaken, Eric and Tom wondered what would happen when they got to the island. Would they be diving for nothing? If so, Tom had promised to give up the search. This whole thing was getting stranger and stranger.

It was more than an hour before they sighted the dome-shaped island surrounded by its bastion of black rocks.

"There it is!" They pointed it out to Walter.

"Good," he said. "Now where's the spot you want to find?"

Remembering the description Ben had given them, Eric directed him to go around the island. "It's a pinnacle of rocks just beyond the shack."

"Here." Kara handed him binoculars. "See if you can find it with these."

In a few minutes, Eric spotted the dilapidated building on the slope not far from a sandy cove. "Right there, on the other side of that rocky peninsula," he said, feeling relieved. At least Ben had described the place accurately.

The goats on the rocks watched as the boat stopped and the anchor went down.

"The depth finder indicates about ninety feet of water," Walter told them.

Eric studied the area. Rocks dotted the shoreline, about fifty yards from the ship. There was still a large area here to search for one sunken boat, but he could see no sign of the sharks Ben had told them were here. However, the water was cloudy. Who could tell what might be down there?

They took turns using the cabin to put on their wetsuits, and when they were all ready, Walter took charge. "We'd better dive in pairs. Eric, why don't you and Tom take the section starting from the boat out to the peninsula. Kara and I can go from here out in the other direction. At ninety feet, our air supply should last about fifteen minutes. We'll meet back here."

"What happens if we sight the *Kelpie?*" Tom asked.

"Go ahead and mark the spot with floats. We have extra air cylinders if we need them."

Eric felt he had been quiet long enough. "Ben Brightstar told us there are sharks here," he said.

"Oh?" His uncle looked concerned. He glanced up at the rocks. "That could be, all right. Goats probably fall in the ocean every now and then—sick or injured ones. That would attract them."

"I'm going to dive anyway," Tom said defensively.

Kara studied the water. "All right. There's no sign of blood or carcasses anywhere that I can see. But why don't we change partners, since you and I are more familiar with sharks, Walter? Tom, you come with me."

Eric strapped on his air cylinder, feeling strangely apprehensive. But none of the others seemed afraid, and he wouldn't be, either. He was just as anxious as Tom to know if the *Kelpie* was really down there.

Kara and Tom dropped over the side of the boat and soon disappeared under the surface. In a moment, Eric and his uncle were dropping into the waves and descending to start their search.

Was it the cold water that made shivers along his arms? Eric tried to relax and let his flippers thrust him deeper, looking into the darkness through his face mask, seeing only an endless black pit below him. Then his eyes accustomed themselves and he saw the twilight world around him. Tiny flashes of silver darted through the gloom as a school of fish went by. A manta ray flapped after them, like a great black bird in a green sky. As they neared the ocean floor, Eric saw that it was covered with flowerlike anemones and starfish, seaweed and shellfish; a jungle of life forms. Fascinated, he followed his uncle's waving flippers, his fears forgotten.

They had searched only a few minutes when Walter turned, grasped Eric's arm, and pointed with his free hand at what looked like a large, encrusted rock just ahead of them. Eric had to look carefully before he realized what it was. A ship! Overgrown with sea-vegetation and layered with shells, the shape of the hull and the cabin were still recognizable. The *Kelpie!* They'd found it!

While his uncle sent up floats to mark the spot, Eric swam around the boat, a thrill of excitement running through him. It stood upright, with only a slight list to port, and he could even see parts of the black letters painted on its stern . . . the straight bar of the "K" and portions of the "e's" as well as the tail of the "p." A few firm swipes of his hand cleared the rest of the "K," but there was no need to see the other letters. Eric knew this must be Steve Kelsey's ship.

He swam toward the cabin, to the place where the door would be. It was gone, the hinges probably corroded away, and there was a cavity yawning darkly. Without hesitating, Eric swam in.

Sea creatures had taken over this part of the ship, too. He moved carefully among the mysterious shapes in the cabin, his hands pulling at them to try to distinguish what they might be. He pushed at an oval lump against a wall. Two eyes gleamed out at him from behind it, then the writhing body of a moray eel flashed past him and was gone. He recoiled, his flipper hitting what once might have been a chair, and saw an octopus scuttle away from it, tentacles waving. He watched it go. It was crawling over something that gleamed whitely in the dimness. When he bent to look closely, two round, empty eyes and a fleshless mouth looked up at him, grinning.

A human skull!

In panic, Eric turned. He had to get out of here! But he was lost. Where had the opening gone? He turned and turned again in helpless terror.

Something black was swimming toward him! Horror chilled through his body until he recognized his uncle, reaching out to grasp his arm, then turning and pulling Eric along with him. Relief shuddered through him. They were out of the cabin, now, and swimming up through the darkness toward the sunlit waters above.

It was then that Eric experienced the strangest sensation he had ever known. He heard a giant whooshing sound over the bubbling of his air exhaust, something like a huge train coming at him, and then he saw a flash of grey-brown passing under him, going so fast that he couldn't see what it was. But somehow, he knew.

It was a shark. The biggest shark in all creation. This was why the underwater world had suddenly become so still. This was why his heart was suddenly pounding in his throat and his breath was tight in his lungs. He strained his ears and eyes, searching frantically below, above, and around him. But the shark had gone. When would it circle back to get them? Why did his body feel like lead, holding him back from the safety of sunlight and air? A moan of dread escaped him, mingled with the small, silent bubbling sound of his breathing, and his uncle's hand on his arm tightened like a steel noose.

15 ● *Jaws of Death*

At last, Eric and his uncle were rising through blue light, the surface only a few feet away. At last they were on top of the waves, and there was the ship, dead ahead of them. Forcing himself to move steadily, knowing that thrashing the water would only attract that shark, Eric followed Walter, who had let go of him as they surfaced. He didn't dare look back now. He could only go steadily forward and hope they would reach the safety of the ship soon.

Soon they were next to the swimming platform at the stern, and now, at last, he was pulling himself out of the water. Uncle Walter climbed up beside him.

It was while they sat there, catching their breath, Eric trying to quiet the pounding of his heart, that they saw Tom and Kara surfacing.

Walter removed his face mask and spoke calmly. "Don't frighten them. Beckon them in."

Eric understood. Panic would only make matters

worse. But he didn't think Kara would panic. He remembered her swimming among those great blues, and shivered in the sunshine. They had been babies compared with the monster that was down there now! He watched, his body tense as Kara and Tom swam lazily toward them, then relieved as he helped them onto the swimming platform. Once they were all clambering onto the deck, he found a chair and collapsed into it.

Tom removed his mouthpiece and face mask. "Did you find anything?"

Eric glanced at his uncle, who was unfastening a shell-encrusted object, about the size of a milk carton, from his belt and setting it on the deck.

"We found the *Kelpie*." Walter straightened and pointed at the floats that were bobbing on the water.

Kara turned to see. "Are you sure?"

"Yes," Eric said. "I saw the name."

Tom gave a triumphant whoop. "We found it! Ben was right!" He danced happily around the deck. "Ben isn't crazy at all! We were right!" He turned suddenly to his mother, who watched him. "And you were wrong, Mom. My dad didn't run away with another woman. He wasn't weak and deceitful. He loved us. He was okay!"

Kara shook her head sadly. "This doesn't prove anything, Tom. There will be two bodies on the boat . . . Steve and his lady friend. We'll get fresh air cylinders and go down and find them. You'll see I'm right." She headed for the cabin, where they'd stowed the diving supplies, but Walter called after her.

"Kara! You can't go near that boat!"

She whirled and stared at him. "Why not?"

"There's a great white shark, a thirteen-footer, cruising around it."

"A great white?" Her eyes widened.

Walter nodded. "It's the biggest one I've ever seen."

She stood silently for a long time, then her chin lifted stubbornly. "I'm going down anyway. I have to see Steve and this Petra woman who was the most important thing in his life. I want to see them both lying down there dead among the fishes. Then I'll know they got what they deserved."

Walter's voice was quiet. "No. I'm not going to let you risk your life."

"You can't tell me what to do!" Her eyes blazed fire at him. "You're just a man—weak and deceitful, like all the rest of them. I hate you . . . all of you!"

Walter looked shaken at this, but his voice was steady. "You know that great whites can be unpredictable, Kara. No matter how experienced you are, don't be foolish. It isn't worth it."

"Oh yes it is. When Steve left me, he took away all the love and trust I could ever give to a man. But sharks aren't like men. They're strong, with the strength of truth. I have a rapport with them. They know I admire them. No shark will hurt me."

"Kara!" Walter called after her, but she had already turned and entered the cabin. In a moment she came out again, fastening on a fresh air cylinder.

"Don't try to follow me," she told them, and then she was over the side of the ship.

"Mom!" Tom gave an anguished cry and ran to see her disappear under the surface of the water.

Walter stood watching the place where she'd disappeared. Then he went into the cabin and brought back a fresh cylinder. As he put it on, he spoke to Tom and Eric. "Stay here. I'll bring her back." He sat on the edge of the deck and went over with a splash.

Tom stood uncertainly for a moment, then darted into the cabin. Eric went after him. "What are you going to do?"

"I've got to help her!"

"But my uncle . . ." His words died out as he saw Tom's face, and knew that nothing could keep him here now. And he couldn't wait here. He knew that. The shark had been the most terrifying thing he'd ever experienced, but there was no way he could let tragedy happen if he could help to stop it. And maybe it would take all of them to stop it. He found another air cylinder and strapped it on.

They went over the side together. Eric felt numb as he swam down through the blue light into the darkness, following Tom's flippers ahead of him. It would be all right. Together, they would all bring Kara back to safety. He clamped his teeth firmly in his mouthpiece and swam steadily, not thinking, not feeling.

Gloom closed in around him. He could barely make out the grey shape of the ship as they swam toward it, but now he could see Kara's slender figure near its prow, and the bigger shape of his uncle, close behind her.

And then, out of nowhere, he heard the noise again, an enormous energy vibrating through the water. Before he could think, he saw Walter's form beside Kara's, clasping his arms around her and propelling her into the cavity of the ship's cabin. At almost the same instant, he saw the giant shark heading for them. Its jaws opened, then closed on the wooden frame of the cabin where the door had been.

Toms' fins thrashed as he stopped his forward motion, Eric behind him. Paralyzed, they crouched on the sea floor and watched the scene not ten feet away from them.

The shark tore at the wood of the ship, breaking pieces away that floated upward. After a moment it maneuvered around where the opening yawned, bigger now that part had been broken off, and thrust its great snout inside.

Eric's heart leaped. But the opening was too small. The shark couldn't get inside. Again and again it attacked the door frame, scattering bits of wood, and Eric knew that it would soon tear the structure apart. He tried to think of something to stop it, but there was no way. They could only watch and pray that somehow, Kara and Walter would escape unharmed.

Seconds passed like hours. It seemed to Eric that he had always stood here, his heart pounding painfully, his body frozen, his thoughts numb. When he saw the cabin collapse slowly, dreamily, in a cloud of debris, he felt his hopes collapse, too. The shark was thrashing through the wreckage. It would find his uncle and Kara now. They were doomed.

The great, sleek body sailed over the ship and around it, and when it turned, Eric saw the great black depths of its cold eyes and the sharp teeth that lined its open jaws. But there was nothing in its mouth, no struggling figure or disembodied limb. How could that be? His numb brain asked the question, but gave no answer. He watched as it turned again, nosing through the broken hull.

And then it moved away. As languidly and indifferently as a great blimp, it swam away from the wrecked ship and disappeared in the darkness.

Eric's numbness drained away. He leaped forward, conscious that Tom was beside him, and together they propelled themselves toward the *Kelpie*.

But something else was moving. A barnacle-covered rectangle rose from the wreckage, pushed up by a black-clad arm. A face mask appeared and a black-hooded head turned from side to side.

It was Walter! Now he was pulling another figure up from a well in the deck, and grasping it about the waist. They were safe! Eric felt no fear now—nothing but thankfulness, as he and Tom followed their companions upward.

They reached the ship safely. Eric and Tom helped Walter as he hoisted Kara, limp and exhausted, to the swimming platform and then onto the deck.

Tom pulled out his mouthpiece. "Are you all right, Mom?"

She weakly removed her face mask. "Yes. I'm all right," and then, while Tom and Eric watched, astonished, she reached up to Walter and put her arms around him. "Thank you," she said. "You saved my life." He held her, smiling. "Well," he said, "we men aren't all that bad."

Eric and Tom busied themselves with taking off their wetsuits. When Kara was seated in a chair at the stern, his uncle beside her, Eric leaned against the rail. "How did you get away from that shark?"

"I found a hatch as quickly as I could," Walter said. "I was sure there had to be one, and there was. We got in there and hid, just before the shark broke through the cabin."

Kara took off her helmet. "I never thought . . . I still can't believe it! A shark, attacking me!"

The bearded man smiled at her. "I hate to say 'I told you so,' but I told you so. That one was out for blood, but they're all unpredictable."

Her smile was feeble. "I'll have to remember that."

Tom was studying the object on the deck. He picked it up. It was covered with shells and seaweed, but Eric could see the gleam of metal through the crust.

"What is it?" he asked.

"I don't know." Tom pried at the shells. "Looks like a metal can of some kind."

"I found that on the *Kelpie*," Walter said.

"The fuel?" Eric was suddenly excited. "Here, let me help."

Together they scraped away the sea animals that coated it, but even before they were through, Eric could see that letters had been scratched into the metal with some kind of tool. He worked at that part of the can until he could read them. When he did, he held the container up toward Kara so that she could see. "There's your Petra," he said.

She stared at the letters on the can. "Petra? He called his *invention* Petra?"

Tom's laugh echoed off the rocks that surrounded them. "Mom! Dad didn't want to leave us! Isn't that great?" He gave her a kiss and a hug, his face glowing with such joy that Eric wanted to laugh with him.

Kara seemed to glow, too. She hugged Tom and smiled at everyone. "I'm so glad. All these years, I thought . . . but I was wrong. It feels as though a weight has been lifted off my heart!" She turned to the man beside her. "Walter, I'm sorry for what I said to you. Can you ever forgive me?"

"Only if you promise to have dinner with me tonight, and let me take you to the concert tomorrow night, and—"

Kara's laugh was musical. "And learn to be friends with human beings again? Of course."

Eric watched them, feeling happy for them and for himself. "But there's still a few questions left," he said to Tom. "Like who killed your dad, and what about that note, and how Al Madow fits into this."

It didn't take them long to find out the answers. Eric told his dad all about it over the phone the next day, with Alison listening on the extension.

"When we got back to the marina, Dad, Al Madow was gone. We looked through the desk in his office and found two more pages to that note he'd given to Kara sixteen years ago. He'd kept them in a special file all this time. It was addressed to Kara, and it was from Steve Kelsey. He said he knew that Al was spying on him, trying to find out the formula for the new fuel he'd invented. It went on to say that Steve was giving the fuel to the government, and the formula was written in an address book in Steve's desk at home. Kara was to turn that over to the officials if anything happened to him."

"But how did Al get the letter?" Alison asked.

"Nobody knows, but Kara suspects he might have taken it from Steve's desk in his den, when he came to their house to comfort her after Steve disappeared. She was so crazy with grief, she never looked for a note."

"Al was stupid to keep it," Dr. Randall Thorne remarked. "But criminals always slip up."

"Right," Eric said. "Al sure did. He was always trying to get back to the Kelsey house to find the formula, but Kara wouldn't let him. Anyway, the police have him now, and he told them everything. It was just about the way Tom and I thought. Al told a big oil company that Steve had invented this new fuel, and they sent out two thugs to help Al get the formula. Those two, Jess and Buck, killed Steve and sank his boat that night before he could meet the government official. Then when Al found out Tom and I were investigating Steve's disappearance, he panicked and set those two creeps after us, to follow us. The thing was that he was so fond of Tom, he told them they'd better not kill us, just scare us off. Then they had to kidnap Ben Brightstar to keep him from telling us what he knew. They were going to leave him on the island until we stopped investigating. They knew we'd have to go back to school sometime."

"And what about the address book?" his father asked. "Is the formula there?"

"Tom and I found it hidden in a drawer. It seems to be in some kind of code. Kara's turning it over to the government. They should be able to figure it out."

"Well," Alison said. "It sounds like you're having a terrible summer, getting mixed up with sharks and criminals and all that."

190

"I forgot to mention that a very pretty girl named Winona has asked us to a party Saturday night," Eric said. "And Tom and I are planning to do a lot of surfing now we have more free time."

"Oh? Well, watch out for sharks," Alison said.

"Sharks?" Eric's tone was superior. "I'm not afraid of sharks. I've dived with big blue sharks, and great white sharks, and I've learned I'm smarter than they are."

"Don't be too confident," his father said. "The Lord God has put many things in this world that cannot be measured or understood by you, or by any human being."

Thorne Twins Adventure Books

by Dayle Courtney

#1—Flight to Terror Eric and Alison's airliner is shot down by terrorists over the African desert (2713).

#2—Escape From Eden Shipwrecked on the island of Molokai in Hawaii, Eric must escape from the Children of Eden, a colony formed by a religious cult (2712).

#3—The Knife With Eyes Alison searches for a priceless lost art form on the Isle of Skye in Scotland (2716).

#4—The Ivy Plot Eric and Alison infiltrate a Nazi organization in their hometown of Ivy, Illinois (2714).

#5—Operation Doomsday Lost while skiing in the Colorado Rockies, the twins uncover a plot against the U.S. nuclear defense system (2711).

#6—Omen of the Flying Light Staying at a ghost town in New Mexico, Eric and Alison discover a UFO and the forces that operate it (2715).

#7—Three-Ring Inferno The twins find jobs with the circus, and must rescue a friend from a motorcycle gang (2892).

#8—Mysterious Strangers Strange look-alikes lead Eric and Alison into a tangle with an international spy ring in Egypt (2893).

#9—The Foxworth Hunt Alison is imprisoned on her uncle's estate, and must find out which of his other guests wants to murder him (2894).

#10—Jaws of Terror Eric must search through shark-infested waters to solve the mystery of his friend's father's disappearance (2895).

#11—The Hidden Cave The twins travel to a tiny island kingdom in the Aegean Sea, where they become involved in a civil war (2896).

#12—Tower of Flames Eric and Alison are trapped inside a building taken over by terrorists (2897).

Available at your Christian bookstore or

STANDARD® PUBLISHING